S0-BRD-850

Grass on the Wayside

Michigan Classics in Japanese Studies, Number 2

Center for Japanese Studies
The University of Michigan

Grass on the Wayside

(Michikusa)

A Novel by Natsume Sōseki

*Translated from the Japanese, and
with an introduction by*
Edwin McClellan

*Center for Japanese Studies, The University of Michigan
Ann Arbor, Michigan*

Library of Congress Cataloging in Publication Data

Natsume, Sōseki, 1867–1916.
   [Michikusa, English]
   Grass on the wayside = Michikusa : a novel / by Natsume Sōseki :
translated from the Japanese and with an introduction by Edwin
McClellan.
       p.   cm.—(Michigan classics in Japanese studies : no. 2)
   Reprint. Originally published: Chicago : University of Chicago
Press, 1969. Originally published in series: UNESCO collection of
representative works. Japanese series.
   ISBN 0–939512–45–9
   I. Title.   II. Series.
PL812.A8M513   1990
895.6'342—dc20   90–1363
                                                           CIP

UNESCO Collection of Representative Works
Japanese Series
This book has been accepted in the Japanese Series of the Translations Collection of the United
Nations Educational, Scientific, and Cultural Organization (UNESCO).

Originally published in Japanese as MICHIKUSA
First edition published by the University of Chicago Press, Chicago and London, 1969
English translation and Introduction © 1969 by UNESCO
All rights reserved

Reprinted with the permission of the University of Chicago Press and UNESCO

Reprinted in 1990 by the Center for Japanese Studies, 108 Lane Hall, The University of
Michigan, Ann Arbor, MI 48109-1290

Printed in the United States of America

*This translation is for
my wife Rachel*

Introduction

I

Natsume Sōseki, with whom the modern realistic novel in Japan reached its full maturity, was born Natsume Kinnosuke in the year 1867 in Tokyo. He later adopted the pen name of Sōseki, which replaced, as is the custom in Japan, his given name.

The Natsumes were a well-established bourgeois family, but after the Imperial Restoration of 1868 their fortunes declined rapidly. When Sōseki was born, his father was fifty-three and his mother forty. There were already other children in the family, all much older than Sōseki. Perhaps because the Natsumes felt they could not afford to bring up another boy, or perhaps because they were embarrassed at having a baby at their age, they soon gave the baby away to a childless couple whom they knew well. That Sōseki could never quite forgive his parents for having done this becomes clear in the novel. And in a reminiscence which he wrote shortly before his death, he has this to say:

I was born to my parents in their evening years. I was their youngest son. The story that my mother was ashamed of having a baby at her age I hear even now.... At any rate, I was sent soon afterward to a certain couple as their adopted son.... I was with them until the age of eight or nine, when one begins to understand things. There was some trouble between them, so it was arranged that I should be returned to my parents.... I did not know that I had come back to my own home and I went on thinking as I did before that my parents were my grandparents. Unsuspectingly I continued to call them "grandma" and "grandpa." They, on their part, thinking perhaps that it would be strange to change things suddenly, said nothing when I called them this. They did not pet me as parents do their youngest children.... I remember particularly that my father treated me rather harshly.... One night, the following incident took place. I was sleeping alone in a room when I was awakened by someone calling my name in a quiet voice. Frightened, I looked at the figure crouching by my bedside. It was dark, so I could not tell who it was. Being a child, I lay still and listened to what the person had to say. Then I realized that the voice belonged to our maid. In the darkness, the maid whispered into my ear: "These people that you think are your grandfather and grandmother are really your father and mother. I am telling you this because recently I heard them saying that you must in some way have sensed that they were your parents, since you seemed to prefer this house to the other one. They were saying how strange it was. You musn't tell anybody that I told you this. Understand?" All I said at the time was "All right," but in my heart I was happy. I was happy not because I had been told the truth, but because the maid had been so kind to me.

But at least, Sōseki's parents cannot have prevented him from getting a decent enough early education, for he entered the University of Tokyo without difficulty and graduated from there in 1893 with a very good degree in English literature. In 1896 he was given an appointment at the Fifth National College at Kumamoto in Kyushu. In the same year he married Nakane Kyōko, whose father was then the Chief Secretary of the House of Peers. (When Sōseki in the novel refers to "the provinces" where he and his wife had lived, he means Kumamoto.) In 1900 the government sent him to England so that he might improve his knowledge of English. He went alone, and spent two unhappy years in London. Upon his return to Japan in 1903, he was appointed to the First National College in Tokyo and the University of Tokyo. In 1905 he published his first full-length novel, *I am a Cat (Wagahai wa neko de aru)*. In 1907 he gave up his academic career, which he had never liked very much, to devote himself to writing. He died in 1916. In all he wrote a dozen novels, of which *Grass on the Wayside (Michikusa)*, his only autobiographical novel, was the last to be completed.

By the time of his resignation from the university, Sōseki had won recognition as a novelist through the publication of two comic novels and a minor lyrical masterpiece, *Pillow of Grass (Kusamakura)*, which he aptly called "a novel in the manner of a haiku." But it was after he stopped teaching that he began to write his most characteristic novels, which are without exception very somber, concerned for the most part with man's loneliness and his effort to escape from it. In *The Gate (Mon)*, one of the most moving of these, the lonely hero goes to a Zen temple in an attempt to find solace in religion, but fails.

He had come to the gate and had asked to have it opened. The bar was on the other side and when he knocked, no one came. He heard a voice saying, "Knocking will do no good. Open it yourself." He stood there and wondered how he could open it. He thought clearly of a plan, but he could not find the strength to put it into effect.... He looked behind him at the path that had led him to the gate. He lacked the courage to go back. He then looked at the great gate which would never open for him. He was never meant to pass through it. Nor was he meant to be content until he was allowed to do so. He was, then, one of those unfortunate beings who must stand by the gate, unable to move, and patiently wait for the day to end.

One Sunday shortly after he returns home from the temple, he goes to the local public bath and overhears two men discussing the weather. They have each heard a nightingale sing and agree that the song was still rather awkward and unpracticed. When he gets home he remembers to tell his wife about the nightingales. She looks at the sun streaming in through the glass window and says cheerfully, "How nice! Spring has finally come." The novel comes to an end as he replies, "Yes, but it will soon be winter again."

When we read the autobiographical *Grass on the Wayside*, we see how much of himself Sōseki had put into the heroes of the preceding novels.

II

Sōseki was a sick man when he wrote *Grass on the Wayside*. After 1910, when he very nearly died from stomach ulcers, he seems to have felt that death was not far away. He wrote the novel in 1915, when he was forty-eight; the following year, before he could complete *Light and Darkness (Meian)*, he died.

The period dealt with in *Grass on the Wayside* is very short. It begins soon after the author's return from London in 1903 and ends as his career as a writer is about to begin. (*I am a Cat* was published in 1905.) Kenzō (the name Sōseki gives himself) is at this time in his middle thirties, and his wife in her middle twenties. It was then, presumably, that relations between Sōseki and his wife became strained and he began to be acutely conscious of his loneliness.

The novel has its shortcomings. It is not devoid of self-pity or naïveté, and it is so introspective that the reader may find it at times rather slow-moving. Nevertheless, it is all in all his most serious work. And of the countless number of autobiographical novels that have been written in Japan since the early 1900's, it is perhaps the most distinguished.

One of the most curious aspects of the history of modern Japanese fiction after the turn of the century is the important place occupied by the autobiographical novel, which was made fashionable by the so-called naturalists who flourished at about the same time as Sōseki. In their attempt to introduce realism into the Japanese novel, these "naturalists" were inclined to regard the novel as a means of describing their own experiences, to think of it more or less as an extended essay form.

Sōseki's conception of realism was not so literal, and much of what is most imaginative and daring in modern Japanese fiction is due largely to his example and influence. In his entire career, he wrote only one autobiographical novel. And when he did, he brought to the genre qualities which had never been seen in it before.

What *Grass on the Wayside* manages to avoid is the rather obvious lyricism of most Japanese autobiographical novels, their annoying reticence and vagueness. Its people are alive and refuse to get lost in the misty Japanese scene. No modern Japanese novelist before Sōseki ever wrote so movingly about his childhood, or created so real a woman as Kenzō's wife. And Kenzō himself remains one of the most fully developed characters in Japanese fiction.

III

Perhaps I ought to say a few things about Japanese family relationships and obligations, since they form such an important part of the novel's background.

The reader will see the ambivalence in Kenzō as he allows himself to become involved with the unpleasant Shimada, who was once his foster father but who now has no legal claim on him whatsoever. Of course, Kenzō is not so inhuman as to want to ignore entirely this man who had once taken care of him. This very human side to Kenzō's feeling about Shimada, his wife and relatives cannot understand. They are more conventional than Kenzō, more legalistic in their attitude: as far as they are concerned, Kenzō, having ceased to be Shimada's adopted son years ago, now owes him nothing. At the same time, they are more frightened of Shimada, for somewhere at the back of their minds is the fear that the law, with its sanction of Confucian principles in the matter of filial obligation, just may support Shimada's claim. They are wrong, of course, and Kenzō knows this. But also, in the guilt that he feels toward Shimada, there is a residue of Confucian morality.

Adoption of the sort described in the novel has for long been a regularly practiced custom in Japan. Indeed, it has been about as important a part of Japanese life, as much of an accepted institution, as marriage. So in giving away Kenzō to Shimada, his parents were not being quite as heartless as it may seem. Or it may be more correct to say that though they were in effect being unkind to their youngest child, they were not doing anything that society would have disapproved of. Formally speaking, Kenzō's father was not getting rid of an unwelcome addition to his already large family, but was granting a favor to a subordinate to whom he, as his superior and past benefactor, owed certain obligations. The subsequent annulment of Kenzō's adoption was very much like a divorce, and an extremely serious affair. And when we remember that Japan is a country where the place of old people in society depends largely on their identity as parents, we can imagine what a blow it was to Shimada.

Lastly, Kenzō's frustration at being surrounded by helpless relatives has to be seen in the light of the great importance attached by the Japanese to their concept of family. His capacity as head of his own household is formally no more important than his membership in the family into which he was born, and as the most successful member, he must assume some responsibility for the welfare not only of his brother and sister but of their respective households too. Such responsibility would seem particularly onerous to a modern individualist like Kenzō, for whom "family" meant his wife and children, and who wanted most of all to be allowed to go his own way.

IV

The original title of this novel is *Michikusa*, the literal meaning of which is "grass on the road." But when used idiomatically, as in *michikusa o kuu*, "to eat grass on the road," it means to waste one's time or to be distracted. The title seems to suggest, therefore, that the novel is about distractions. But perhaps Sōseki intended it to be understood in another sense, that his private life had been that of an outsider, like a weed growing beside the main road.

The book is divided into one hundred and two chapters. This is because, like so many other famous modern Japanese novels, it was first serialized in a newspaper—in this case the *Asahi shimbun*.

EDWIN McCLELLAN

Grass on the Wayside

1

EXACTLY how many years, Kenzō wondered, had he been away from Tokyo? He had left the city to live in the provinces and then had gone abroad. There was novelty in living in his native city once more; but there was some loneliness in it too.

The smell of the alien land that he had left not so long ago seemed still to linger about his body. He detested it, and told himself he had to get rid of it. That he was also rather proud of it, that it gave him a certain sense of accomplishment, he did not know.

Dutifully, and with the uneasiness of the recently returned exile, Kenzō would walk day after day from his house in Komagome to his place of work and back.

A light rain was falling steadily the day it happened. With only an umbrella to shield him from the rain, he was walking at the usual time, along the usual route, toward Hongō. It was just beyond the rickshaw stand that the unexpected encounter took place. The other man had presumably come up the hill behind the Nezu Gongen shrine. He was perhaps twenty yards away when Kenzō, happening to raise his eyes, first saw him approaching. Quickly Kenzō looked away.

He wanted to pretend he had not recognized him. But as the man came nearer, he felt he had to look at him again to make sure he had not been mistaken. He looked, and found the man staring at him.

The street was quiet at the time. Through the fine, almost invisible drizzle they could see each other clearly. Again Kenzō averted his glance and walked on. The man stood absolutely still and stared in silence as Kenzō walked past. Kenzō noticed, out of the corner of his eye, that with every step he took the man's face moved a little.

Kenzō could not have been any more than twenty when they had last met. For fifteen, perhaps sixteen years, they had not seen each other.

In that time, his own position in life had changed so much. He saw himself as he was now, with his moustache and bowler hat; am I, he wondered, the same person as that young innocent fellow with the close-cropped hair? But the man in the street seemed hardly to have changed at all. Surely he must be at least sixty-five by now. But his hair was as black as ever. And he was still walking about hatless, as he always had done. The lack of physical change in him made Kenzō strangely apprehensive.

Kenzō had not wanted to see him, of course. And he had always hoped that if by some chance they were to run into each other, the man would at least appear more prosperous than himself. But anyone would have immediately guessed that he was not in easy circumstances. His not wearing a hat—well, that could be dismissed as an idiosyncracy. It was his shabby clothes that bothered Kenzō. Even his umbrella was made of some cheap, heavy-looking sateen. At best he seemed an ageing, lower middle-class townsman engaged in some dull occupation.

All that day Kenzō tried in vain to forget him. Even at home that evening he felt pursued by those staring eyes. He said nothing about it to his wife, however. It was always his habit when upset to say very little to her. She, too, when her husband was in this sort of mood, would say no more than was necessary.

2

*T*HE next day Kenzō walked up the same street at the same hour. And again the next day. For five days, like an unfailing machine, he went back and forth. But the man did not appear.

Then, on the sixth day, he suddenly appeared once more, like a threatening shadow from the hill behind the shrine. The hour was the same, and they would pass each other almost on the same spot.

Kenzō sensed the man's desire to accost him and took care not to slacken his steady pace. This time the man was more bold. With a terrible concentration he fixed his dull, tired eyes on

Kenzō. He was watching for an opening, for some sign of relenting in Kenzō. Kenzō walked past, with all the nonchalance he could muster. He thought fearfully, this is only the beginning. That evening again, he could not bring himself to mention the man to his wife.

When he married her—which was about seven or eight years ago—he had long ceased to have anything to do with him. Besides, they had married in the provinces, so she could hardly have had any opportunity of meeting him. Of course, she might have heard about him from relatives or from Kenzō himself. But the question of whether or not his wife knew of his existence was really of little importance.

There was one incident, however, which had taken place after their marriage, that he remembered periodically. One day about five years ago, when he was still working in the provinces, a thick envelope addressed to him in a woman's hand was placed on his desk at the office. With some uneasiness he began to read the letter. It was incredibly long—twenty pages packed with very small handwriting—and after reading about a fifth of it he gave up He took it home with him and handed it to his wife. He felt obliged to explain to her who this woman was that had written him such a long letter. And in so doing he could not avoid bringing the man into the picture.

He remembered quite clearly now that it had been necessary then to mention him. But he was aware of his own capriciousness, and he had no notion now of how much he might have told her. No doubt his wife would remember exactly what he had said at the time. But he was not inclined at this point to ask her how much she remembered. At any rate, he thoroughly disliked having to think of the woman who had written the letter in association with the man. For to think of them together was to bring back the unhappy past.

Fortunately he was too busy to allow himself to remain preoccupied with such matters. He changed his clothes as soon as he got home and immediately went into his tiny study. The thought of all the work that was waiting to be done constantly oppressed him. It was not the kind of work he would have chosen to do, he felt; consequently, he was always in a state of nervous irritation. He thought of the time when he first opened the crates of books he had brought back from abroad. For two weeks he had simply left the English books lying in untidy piles all over the floor of this cramped study, and had sat in their midst doing nothing. He would pick up a book at random and read two or three pages, then put it down and pick up another. The books would have remained on the floor indefinitely had not a friend, who could not stand the mess any longer, simply decided one day to put them on the shelves himself. Of course, there was no order whatsoever to the way he arranged the books. Many people who knew Kenzō said that he was suffering from some kind of nervous breakdown. But he believed that it was simply his nature to behave this way.

3

KENZŌ was always busy. So much work was being forced on him that not a day went by when he did not feel harried. Even at home he could not allow himself to relax for a moment. Besides, there were all those books he wanted to read; and he needed time to think, to write the kind of things he wanted to write. His mind no longer knew what it was like to rest.

That he might leave his desk once in a while and indulge in some sort of recreation never occurred to him. A well-meaning friend once suggested that he might take up Nō recitation as a hobby. He had grace enough to refuse politely, but secretly he was quite shocked at the man's frivolity. How can the fellow, he asked himself incredulously, find the time for such nonsense? He could not see that his own attitude toward time had become mean and miserly.

He was forced by circumstances to cut himself off from the company of other men. His loneliness as a human being increased as his mind became more and more occupied with the written word. At times he was vaguely aware of his loneliness. And he knew that his way of life must seem arid to others. But he was confident that it was the proper one for him, that no matter how outwardly desolate his daily existence might become, the passion deep inside him would not wither away.

His relatives regarded him as an eccentric. This did not bother him. "After all," he would say to his wife, "they haven't had my education." And his wife would retort, "You've got a swelled head, that's your trouble."

Unhappily, Kenzō was not quite able to ignore such comments from his wife. He would feel not only irritation but disgust at her lack of understanding. Sometimes he would get really angry and scold her into silence. But this did no good. She would simply take his bad temper as just another indication of his vanity. Quite unrepentant, she would go away thinking what a pompous windbag she had married.

He had only two close blood relatives, an elder brother and an elder half-sister. Unfortunately he had little contact even with these two. Sometimes he felt it was not quite right of him to ignore them as he did. But in the end there was no doubt in his mind that his work was far more important than keeping in constant touch with them. Besides, the fact that he had seen them three or four times after returning to Tokyo eased his conscience a little.

Had he not come upon that man, he would have kept to his normal routine and stayed at home the following Sunday, either at his desk or lying in exhaustion on the floor of his study. But that Sunday, as he began thinking of the man again, he decided he would visit his sister for a change.

She lived on a small sidestreet in Yotsuya. She had married a cousin, roughly the same age as herself. They were many years older than Kenzō. The husband had at one time been employed at the local ward office, and though he did not work there any more, they continued to live in their shabby house in Yotsuya. "It's awkward for my husband, I know," she would explain, "but you see, our friends all live around here."

4

*T*HE sister suffered from asthma. She was an extremely restless woman, however, and only a most severe attack of it would keep her still. All day long she rushed about the house, wheezing away, in search of something to do. Her restlessness seemed to Kenzō quite undignified and somehow pitiful.

She was a great talker. Moreover, there was not a hint of breeding in her speech. After a few minutes of her company Kenzō would invariably become silent and disapproving. And he would tell himself bitterly, "This woman, alas, is my sister."

When he reached the house, he found her with her sleeves tucked up, cleaning out the cupboard. "What a surprise," she said. "Sit down and make yourself comfortable." She pushed a cushion toward him, then went away to wash her hands.

Kenzō looked around the room. On the latticework above the door hung a framed piece of calligraphy. He remembered his brother-in-law telling him—it must have been fifteen years ago—that it was very good calligraphy, that it was by someone who had been a retainer of the Shogun. Despite the considerable difference in age between them, the brother-in-law had allowed Kenzō to treat him like a brother. He remembered how they used to wrestle like children in the house, much to the annoyance of his sister. Once they had climbed onto the roof and, sitting there, gorged themselves on figs. The next-door neighbor was furious when he discovered that they had thrown the skins into his yard. And how he had sulked when his brother-in-law failed to produce the compass in a wooden box that he had promised him. He remembered too the time when he had that bitter quarrel with his sister. He was determined never to forgive her. He waited expectantly nevertheless for her to come to him with apologies. When she did not appear, he swallowed his pride and decided he would have to go to see her. Feeling very foolish he had stood awkwardly outside her house until she called out, "Why don't you come in?"

As Kenzō gazed at the calligraphy and thought of the couple who had been so good to him, he began to wish, with some bitterness, that he could feel more affection for them now.

"And how are you these days?" he said to his sister as she sat down in front of him. "The asthma is still giving you trouble, I suppose."

"I'm all right, don't you worry. The weather's been quite decent, thank goodness. I can still do the housework, as you see. Mind you, I'm not young any more, and I can't rush around the way I used to. I was a real worker in those days, wasn't I? Why, I used to scrub the outside of all my pots and pans. I'm not up to that sort of thing now, I can tell you. But of course, I drink milk every day, thanks to you. . . ."

Kenzō was then sending her a small monthly allowance. "You seem to have lost a little weight," he said.

"I've always been thin, Kenzō. I've never been fat in my life. I'm the nervous type, and you can't get fat on nerves."

She rolled up her sleeve, and stuck out her skinny arm. Beneath her large, sunken eyes loose folds of dark skin hung lifelessly. In silence Kenzō looked at the dry palm of her hand.

"But what a good thing you've turned out to be such a success," she was saying. "You know, when you went abroad, I really didn't think I would see you again. But here you are, safe and sound. How happy father and mother would have been to see you as you are now!"

She was becoming tearful. With some amusement Kenzō remembered the boisterous woman he had known as a child. "When I get rich," she would say if in a good mood, "I'll buy you anything you like." Or, if annoyed, "You pigheaded child, you'll never amount to anything."

5

KENZŌ looked at his sister and thought, she really has aged since then. He said, "By the way, how old are you?"

"Fifty-one. Pretty ancient, eh?" She smiled, showing her yellow, straggly teeth.

Kenzō had not expected her to be quite so old. "I had completely forgotten," he said. "I was under the impression that you were at most ten years older than I."

"Don't be silly. There's a difference of sixteen years between us. Let's see now—my husband is the year of the sheep, and three blue; I'm four green, and I'm sure you're seven red."

"I've no idea what you're talking about. All I know is that I'm thirty-six."

"Look up your horoscope. You're seven red, you'll see."

Kenzō had no notion of how one went about looking up one's horoscope. He decided to change the subject. "Where's Hida?" he asked.

"He was on night duty again last night. Actually, he really doesn't have to go on night duty more than two or three times a month. But his colleagues are always asking him to take their place. Besides, we can always use the extra pay. I suppose he spends as many nights away as he does at home—maybe more."

Kenzō said nothing, and looked at Hida's desk in the corner. Arranged very neatly on it were inkstand, envelopes, and writing paper, and next to these stood three ledgers with red-leather backs. At the foot of the ledgers lay a small, shining abacus.

Kenzō had heard that Hida was having an affair with some trollop and that he had set her up near his place of work. Kenzō wondered how many of Hida's nights away were passed in the company of his mistress. "How is Hida these days? He must surely have become less frivolous in his old age."

"Not at all. He has always had just one purpose in life, and that's to have fun. As long as the money lasts, he spends all his time going to vaudeville shows, the theater, wrestling matches, and so on. One odd thing about him though—he does seem to have become somewhat gentler. Perhaps that's a sign of old age, I don't know. You remember how violent he used to be—beating and kicking me, dragging me around the room by the hair. . . ."

"You weren't exactly passive yourself."

"What do you mean? I never laid a hand on him. Never."

Kenzō could not help smiling. The fights these two used to have were by no means one-sided. And when it came to a verbal battle, Hida was no match for her. It struck Kenzō as pathetic that this once high-spirited woman should now be so ready to believe her husband's lies. "Let me take you out somewhere to eat," he said.

"Thanks, but I've already arranged to have some sushi brought over, so we'll stay here, if that's all right with you. The sushi is nothing special, mind you."

Whatever the time of day, no guest was ever allowed to leave her house without having had some food forced down his throat. Kenzō decided he might as well resign himself to staying for a while; besides, he really did want to talk to her about the other matter.

6

*P*ERHAPS because of overwork and mental fatigue, his stomach was giving him trouble these days. On very few occasions, when he was feeling particularly optimistic, he had tried exercising, but this had only increased the heaviness around and below his chest. Now he was merely taking the precaution of eating nothing besides his three main meals a day.

"Don't worry," his sister said. "It's only plain sushi. You'll be all right. I got it especially for you, so I'll be very hurt if you don't eat it. You do like it, don't you?"

In the face of this brutal insistence Kenzō had no choice but to give in. Reluctantly he put one of the tasteless lumps into his nicotine-coated mouth and began to chew laboriously.

She continued to chatter. To be forced into silence when he had something to say to her annoyed him considerably. But she was too insensitive to notice.

Giving things away to her guests afforded her as much pleasure as seeing them eat. She was now offering him the moth-eaten picture of Dharma that he had unwittingly praised during a previous visit.

"It's of no use to us. By all means take it. Hida won't mind. What would he do with a shabby thing like that anyway?" Kenzō smiled, and refused to commit himself. She then lowered her voice conspiratorially and said, "There's a certain matter I've been wanting to talk to you about ever since you got back. I knew you were busy, and I didn't want to ask you to come out here just to listen to my problems. I might have come to your house, I suppose, but I really couldn't talk about it in front of your wife. And you know how difficult it is for me to write letters."

There was a touch of comedy, Kenzō thought, in her long, solemn preamble. From early childhood she had had a hopeless memory for characters, and even now, at the age of fifty, she was incapable of writing the simplest sentence literately. He was sorry for her; but he was also a little ashamed of her. He said, "What is it that you want to tell me? I have something to tell you myself."

"Is that so? In that case, let's hear what you have to say first. Why in the world didn't you speak up sooner?"

That her own garrulousness would prevent others from talking was a fact she had always managed to ignore. He said, "I haven't been able to put a word in edgewise."

"You could have interrupted me, you know," she said. "No need for politeness between brother and sister, that's my motto!"

"Quite so. Well, I'm ready to listen."

"It's terribly difficult for me to say this, but as you know, I'm getting older and weaker, and you know what my husband is like—he is happy so long as he himself is all right, he doesn't care how I am. Besides, he doesn't make very much money, and he has certain social obligations. You could say it's none of your business, and you would be right, of course. . . ."

Kenzō wished women wouldn't be so devious. Why couldn't she say what she wanted to say and be done with it? She was asking for more money, obviously. He had heard that the allowance he was already sending her often went into her husband's pocket. He tried hard not to be angry, reminding himself that it was all very sad really.

She ended her entreaty with these words: "Do say you'll help your sister. This poor little body isn't going to last much longer anyway."

Kenzō could not bring himself to refuse.

7

THERE was work he had to do that night. His sister was the sort to whom time meant absolutely nothing, and he could not go on forever listening to her chatter. He decided to leave at the first opportune moment. But he had to mention the man before he left. "I bumped into Shimada the other day," he began.

"Really! Where?" This was said in almost a shriek. Like so many uneducated Tokyo women, she was given to dramatics.

"Near Otanohara."

"Why, that's near where you live. What did he do? Did he say anything?"

"Hardly. He wasn't given the chance."

"Quite right. It would have been real cheek if he had spoken to you first."

It seemed to Kenzō that she was doing her best to say what she thought he wanted to hear. She was not entirely without pity for Shimada, however, when she was told that he had been shabbily dressed. "He can't be having a very easy time, then," she said.

She started reminiscing about him, and her tone once more became vindictive. "Now, there's the meanest man I've ever seen. I remember him sitting here, refusing to budge. He wouldn't listen to any of my excuses, and kept on insisting that payment was overdue and he wasn't going without it. Finally, I lost my temper and told him I didn't have a penny, but if he didn't mind being paid in kind, he could take my iron cooking-pot. And do you know what the so-and-so said? 'All right,' he said, 'I'll take it.' I was flabbergasted, I can tell you."

"But surely, the cooking-pot must have been far too heavy for him to carry away?"

"Don't you believe it. That man is capable of anything. What he had in mind, of course, was to make us go without rice that day. So he's having a hard time now, eh? It serves him right."

Her account of the ludicrous incident failed to amuse Kenzō. After all, he thought sadly, I play a part in all this, I cannot forget my own past. "I saw him twice, you know," he said. "It's likely I'll see him again."

"Keep on ignoring him, that's all, no matter how often you see him."

"It's possible that he was going somewhere, and we met accidentally. But don't you think that he might actually have been looking for me?"

She had no answer. She kept on talking inanities. It became increasingly clear to Kenzō that all she was trying to do was to flatter and soothe him.

"Has he come here at all since then?" he asked.

"No, he hasn't shown up for the last two or three years."

"And before that?"

"He used to come occasionally, not often. And do you know, he always dropped in at about eleven in the morning. I couldn't get rid of him until he'd been fed. Eel casserole, and that sort of thing. I suppose he couldn't bear to miss the chance of a free meal. But he can't have been stingy about his clothes—he was always nattily turned out in those days."

She was flying off on a tangent again. But at least Kenzō did gather from all she was saying that after he had left Tokyo, she and Shimada had continued to meet to discuss money matters. Other than this, he could find out nothing from her.

8

"IS Shimada still living in the old house?" he asked. His sister could not answer even this simple question. He was surprised; he had expected her to know at least that much about Shimada. Of course, he was not particularly anxious to know. If after this, he told himself, he did try to find out where Shimada lived, it would be simply out of curiosity; and this kind of idle curiosity was a luxury a busy man like himself could not afford.

He could still remember very clearly Shimada's house where he had lived as a child.

It faced a wide moat that was over a hundred yards long. The water in the moat was quite stagnant. Sometimes patches of green scum would appear on the surface, giving out an evil stench. On the other side stood a great mansion belonging to some nobleman. Lined up alongside the outer stone wall was a row—it looked endless—of retainers' houses. Each of these houses, he remembered, had one square window, dark and forbidding. The mansion itself was completely hidden from view.

Modest bungalows of assorted shapes and sizes, separated here and there by empty lots, stood on his side of the moat. They looked rather like an old man's teeth.

Shimada had bought himself a small piece of land there and built his house—exactly when, Kenzō did not know. But he remembered that it was still new when he went to live with Shimada. It was tiny, with only four rooms. But to his boyish eyes it seemed to have been built with care and taste. The rooms were well arranged. The six-mat living room faced the east, and overlooked a small garden covered with pine needles. One corner of the garden was dominated by an incongruously grand stone lantern.

Shimada was a man of neat habits. He seemed always to be polishing the wooden floor of the verandah with a wet cloth, or pulling out the weeds in the yard on the south side of the house, or cleaning out the ditch by the front gate with a hoe.

Next to this house Shimada built an even smaller one to rent. Between the two houses was an alley which led to an open field at the back. Actually it was more of a swamp than a field. There was not a dry spot anywhere. Indeed, the hollow parts were so full of water that they might quite properly have been called ponds. It was apparently Shimada's intention to build another house to rent in this part of the property, but he never did. "Wild duck come down here in the winter," he once said to Kenzō. "I'll catch one for you."

How changed the place must be, Kenzō thought. Yet somehow he could not quite believe that everything would not be exactly as it was twenty years ago.

"It's possible that Hida sent him a card last New Year," his sister said. She was trying to persuade him to stay until her husband returned. Kenzō, however, did not think it necessary to wait for him simply to find out Shimada's address.

He had originally intended to go to his brother's house afterward, partly to see how he was and partly to ask him about Shimada. But it was getting late; besides, his brother was not likely to know very much. He decided to go straight home.

That night he immersed himself in work that had to be done by the next day. Shimada was completely forgotten.

9

H_E returned once more to his usual routine, and found himself able to devote most of his energy to his work. The hours passed quietly for the most part. Yet he felt beset by one worry after another. His wife remained aloof and watched him from afar. She had long ago decided that she could do nothing to comfort him. Her seeming indifference angered Kenzō. Had she forgotten she was his wife? She, on her part, reasoned that if he was content to spend all his time in the study, then she was not to blame for their estrangement.

She left him alone with his books and came to seek the company only of their children. The children too left him alone. Sometimes they were allowed to come into the study, but such visits always ended in disaster. Kenzō knew that his children were now staying away from him because of his bad temper. It was not their fault, but still, he was disappointed.

The following Sunday he stayed in his house. At about four in the afternoon he had a hot bath, in the hope that this might change his mood. He felt surprisingly relaxed when he came out. He lay down on the floor and fell into a very deep sleep. When his wife came in to announce dinner, he was still lying there like a man in a coma.

He went to the table feeling refreshed, but as soon as he sat down he began to feel a slight chill down his back. He sneezed violently, twice. His wife, sitting beside him, said nothing. Neither did he, but he resented her lack of concern. She remained silent, hating his pride and reserve, and thinking: it's his fault that I can't behave like a wife.

Later that evening he decided he had a cold. He knew he should go to bed early, but work kept him up till midnight. The rest of the family had all gone to sleep. Had his wife been awake, he would have asked for some hot gruel to make him sweat. Resignedly he crept into his cold bed. He felt thoroughly chilled and at first found it difficult to go to sleep. But he was much too exhausted to stay awake for long.

When he awoke the next morning, he felt rested. He wondered whether he had shaken the cold off after all. In the bathroom, however, the usual rubdown with cold water proved a great ordeal. Every muscle in his body seemed to have gone limp. Martyr-like he forced himself to appear at the breakfast table. He could not enjoy the food. He had only one bowl of rice instead of the usual three. He put a pickled plum in his empty bowl, then poured hot tea over it. Noisily and ostentatiously he began to sip the brew. Had he been asked why he was doing this, he would have been at a loss for an answer. His wife watched him quietly. Again he became irritated at her aloofness, which seemed particularly calculated this morning. He coughed loudly two or three times for her benefit. But she was quite unmoved.

He changed into his Western clothes quickly and was ready to leave the house at the usual time. As always, his wife came to the front hall to hand him his hat and see him off. She's very careful to observe the formalities, he thought bitterly.

The chill persisted all day. His tongue felt heavy and dry, his whole body seemed dulled with fever. Once, in his office, he felt his pulse, and was shocked. The quick beat registered itself almost audibly on his fingertips. He could hear too the loud ticking of his pocket watch. Fearfully he listened to the macabre duet.

He pulled himself together and went on with his work.

10

*W*HEN he got home his wife appeared with his lounging clothes and stood by, waiting to help him change. Sourly he looked away. "Get my bed ready," he said, "I'm going to lie down."

He made no reference to his cold. And she behaved as though nothing was the matter with him. Privately each found the other's conduct unforgivable.

He was dozing when she came to his bedside and said, "Will you have dinner?"

"Of course not."

She would not go away. After a while she said, "Aren't you feeling well?"

Instead of replying he pulled up the quilt until it covered half his face. Gently she placed her hand on his forehead to feel his temperature.

That evening, after the doctor had left, she gave Kenzō the medicine. Apparently he had nothing more than a cold.

His fever was worse next morning. Following the doctor's instructions, she put a rubber icebag on his forehead and held it there until the maid came back from the hardware store with a nickel-plated suspender for the bag.

He was delirious for two days. On the third day the fever left him. He opened his eyes, feeling quite recovered, and stared at the ceiling blankly. Then he looked at his wife; and he suddenly realized that she had been taking care of him. Without saying a word to her he turned his face away. In doing this, he lost his chance of telling her how he really felt.

"What's the matter with you now?" she said.

"According to the doctor, I've caught a cold."

"Thank you for telling me."

The conversation ended there. In disgust she left the room. Kenzō clapped his hands to summon her back.

"All right," he said, "what's wrong?"

"I sat here for two days looking after you. And all you could say during that time was 'go away, leave me alone.' It's too much. . . ." She stopped abruptly.

"I don't remember saying anything like that to you."

"I don't suppose you do, since you were delirious. But if

you truly didn't feel that way, you wouldn't have said it, no matter how ill you were."

On such occasions as this, it was Kenzō's habit to argue his wife down. It never occurred to him to wonder whether there was not some truth in whatever she was saying.

Once again, he proved her mistaken—at least theoretically. He insisted that when delirious, or when under the influence of drugs, or when having a nightmare, a man might say all kinds of things he really didn't mean. But she was not convinced.

"Have it your own way," she said. "I'm used to being treated like a maid. All you care about is yourself."

Angrily he stared at her back as she walked away. He had not the slightest suspicion that in winning an argument one might end up fooling oneself as well as the opponent. And no doubt from the standpoint of a trained academic like himself, his wife's refusal to listen to reason was quite inexcusable.

11

THAT night his wife came in with a pot of rice gruel and sat down beside him. She ladled some into a bowl and said, "Why don't you try to sit up."

His whole mouth was furry and swollen, and he had no desire to eat. Yet for some reason he sat up obediently and reached for the bowl. The few grains of rice in the liquid felt rough and very large as they passed over his tongue. He could taste nothing. After one helping—it was all he could manage—he lay down.

"Aren't you hungry?" she asked.

"I can't taste a thing."

She brought out a visiting card and gave it to him. "I had the maid tell him you were too ill to see anybody."

Kenzō failed to recognize the name. "When did he come?"

"It must have been the day before yesterday. I wanted to mention it to you sooner, but I thought I'd better wait until your fever went down."

"I don't know the man at all."

"He apparently told the maid he came to see you about Shimada."

She looked questioningly at him. Kenzō thought that "Shimada" had been said with undue emphasis. The image of the hatless figure standing in the middle of the road flashed through his mind. For some days now he had managed to forget the man. "Do you know about Shimada?" he asked.

"You once talked to me about him. It was when you got the long letter from that woman—Otsune was her name, I remember."

Kenzō said nothing. He picked up the card and looked at it again. He wondered how much he had told her then. "When was that?" he asked. "It was a long time ago, surely." He smiled wryly to himself as he remembered how he had felt when he showed his wife the letter.

"Let me see—it would be about seven years ago. We were still living in Senpendōri then." She was referring to a suburb of a provincial town. "I have also heard about him from your brother."

"What did he tell you?"

"Well, among other things, that he wasn't a particularly nice man. Is that true?"

She seemed to want to hear more about Shimada, but Kenzō broke off the discussion by closing his eyes. Taking the hint, she picked up the tray with the pot and bowl on it and stood up. "By the way," she said, "the man told the maid he would like to come again when you were better."

Kenzō was forced to open his eyes. "Of course he'll come. So long as he is acting as Shimada's emissary, he's bound to come."

"But are you going to see him if he does? Surely it would be better not to." She sounded almost adamant.

Kenzō did not want to see him at all, but he said, "Why shouldn't I see him? I'm not frightened of him."

He's being perverse again, she thought. Kenzō knew what she was thinking. But as far as he was concerned, he had no choice. It was only proper that he should receive the stranger when he came; whether he wanted to or not was irrelevant.

12

KENZŌ recovered quickly and found no difficulty in getting back to his daily routine. He read and scribbled in his study for some days without interruption. Then the stranger who had tried to see him when he was ill showed up again without warning.

He took the visiting card from his wife and looked at it. It was made of the same heavy paper, and the name, Yoshida Torakichi, was now familiar. Almost in a whisper his wife said, "Are you going to see him?"

"Yes, I am. Show him to the living room."

She hesitated, but sensing her husband's mood, she left the study obediently.

Yoshida turned out to be a well-built, impressive-looking fellow of about forty, dressed rather dashingly in Japanese clothes. His jacket was of natty striped stuff, and the casually tied sash around his kimono was of white crepe. A glittering watch chain hung from the sash. Not only his clothes but his speech indicated that he was a downtown type. Yet no one would take him for one of those strait-laced city merchants. There was something too eager, too theatrical, about his manner.

Kenzō had decided that it would be entirely proper for him to ask the visitor exactly who he was. But the glib Yoshida needed no prompting; without being asked, he began at once to explain himself.

He used to live in Takahashi, he said. His business then was to supply the army barracks there with provisions. "I had the honor," he said, "to come to know the officers quite well. Yes indeed, the gentlemen were very kind—particularly Mr. Shibano."

Kenzō recognized the name. The daughter of Shimada's second wife, he now remembered, had married a soldier named Shibano. "So that is how you know Shimada," he said.

They talked for a while about Shibano. He had left Takahashi some years back, Yoshida said, for a post farther west. He had continued to drink heavily and was having money trouble. All this was news to Kenzō, but it was of no particular interest to him.

He bore no ill will toward the Shibanos. He sat and waited politely for Yoshida to get down to business. At last Yoshida began to talk about Shimada.

With mounting distaste Kenzō listened to Yoshida's repeated

references to Shimada's poverty. "He's such a decent, trusting fellow," Yoshida said, "he's constantly being cheated. Lord knows how many wild ventures he's been talked into backing."

"Perhaps," Kenzō suggested, "he's just greedy." He found it impossible to believe that the old man had become poor because of his good nature. Indeed, he doubted very much that he was poor at all.

Yoshida seemed not in the least offended by Kenzo's suggestion. "You may be right," he said, and laughed. But the next moment he blandly asked Kenzō if he would agree to send Shimada some money every month.

Kenzō was by nature without guile. To this stranger he began to explain in great detail the exact state of his finances. He pointed out that his monthly salary was a hundred and twenty yen, which was barely enough to make ends meet. He described his various expenses, and tried hard to convince the visitor that at the end of the month not a penny of his salary remained. Yoshida listened solemnly, occasionally throwing in sympathetic comments in his stagy way. But Kenzō wondered how much of his lengthy explanation was really being believed.

He detected not the slightest hint of aggressiveness in Yoshida's manner. Here's a smooth customer, he thought; he's going to play the humble petitioner to the end.

13

KENZŌ, thinking that no further discussion was necessary, waited for his guest to get up and go. He was disappointed. Yoshida did not mention money again, true, but he showed no sign of going, and continued to talk idly about matters of no interest to Kenzō. After a while, however, he manipulated the conversation back to the subject of Shimada. "He's getting on in years, as you know, and he's beginning to feel rather lonely and helpless. I wonder, would it be at all possible for you to associate with him as you used to?"

Kenzō did not quite know what to say. He looked at the tobacco tray he had placed in front of the visitor, and thought of the old man with the shoddy umbrella staring at him through the rain. Kenzō could not helping hating him. He remained silent, torn between his sense of indebtedness and his hatred.

Yoshida's manner became even more ingratiating. "I am sure you will understand, sir, that I should like to feel that my visit has not been entirely in vain. Please, do say yes."

Kenzō reluctantly admitted to himself that no matter how repugnant the prospect of associating with Shimada might be, it would be wrong to refuse to see him at all. "All right, Mr. Yoshida," he said, "please tell him I've agreed to see him. But it's no use pretending that our relationship hasn't changed. Please make sure that he knows this. Also, I want to tell you now that I won't have the time to visit him simply to console him."

"I take it, then, that he may occasionally come here?"

It pained Kenzō to imagine Shimada dropping in regularly for a chat. He could not bring himself to answer Yoshida's question.

"I understand perfectly," Yoshida said. "It's very kind of you. I am quite satisfied. Of course I realize that circumstances have changed."

Yoshida appeared to feel that his mission had been accomplished. He picked up the tobacco pouch he had toyed with throughout the interview and stuck it in his sash. He was now in a hurry to be off.

Kenzō saw Yoshida to the gate, then returned to his study. He wanted to finish the day's work quickly. But he felt restless and irritable, and could not keep his mind on what he was doing. Once his wife came to the door and said, "May I come in?" He pretended not to hear, and went on working. She walked away. He remained in the study until evening, accomplishing very little.

They sat down to dinner later than usual. Now was her chance to ask questions. "Who exactly is that man Yoshida?"

"He apparently used to trade with the army in Takahashi."

Kenzō could hardly hope to satisfy his wife's curiosity with this meager piece of information. What did Yoshida have to do with Shibano, she wanted to know, and what was Yoshida's connection with Shimada? "No doubt he asked for money."

"Quite right."

"Well, what did you say? You did refuse, didn't you?"

"Yes, I did. What else could I do?"

They sat quietly for a while, each thinking of money. What he made was barely enough for them to live on, and it was an immense struggle for him to make even that much. It was no less easy for her, who had to keep the house going on so little.

14

KENZŌ was about to leave the table when his wife began to ask more questions. "Do you mean to say that that man meekly went away when you refused? I find that a little odd."

"What would you have expected him to do? Pick a fight with me, perhaps?"

"I'm sure he's going to come back. I don't care how well-behaved he was today, he's going to come back."

"Let him, if he wants to. Who cares?"

"But I don't like it. I don't want horrid men like that hanging around."

Kenzō realized at last that his wife had been eavesdropping on him and Yoshida. "Why, you heard everything we said, didn't you?" She looked noncommittal. "If you know everything," he said, once more preparing to leave the table, "why bother me with all these questions?"

Kenzō hated to have others pry into his private affairs. He was under no obligation, he felt, to explain to his wife anything that did not concern her directly.

She had learned to pay lip service to her husband's insistence on privacy. Inwardly, however, she never stopped resenting it. She could hardly be expected to take kindly to his overbearing aloofness. Why, she would always ask herself, can't he be a little more open with me? It never crossed her mind, of course, that had she possessed more tact, he might indeed have been more friendly.

"I thought I heard you say that you would see Shimada."

"That's right," he said. His look suggested it was none of her business. Usually at such a point in the conversation she would retreat into silence, and Kenzō, seeing her ill-concealed resentment, would become even more antagonistic. "It has nothing to do with you or your relatives," he added. "I'll handle my own affairs in any way I see fit. Don't worry about matters that don't concern you."

"Go ahead and do what you like. You never did care how I felt about anything."

What an ignorant woman, he thought, she's rambling again; more schooling would have taught her to stick to the point.

Her next remark, however, forced him to take her somewhat

more seriously: 'Father would not approve of your associating with that man, you know."

"Father? Whose father? You're not by any chance referring to my father?"

"You know very well I'm referring to your father."

"But he's been dead a long time!"

"I was told that before he died he said that he had formally broken with Shimada, and that you were not to have anything more to do with him."

Kenzō remembered only too well the final quarrel that led to the severing of relations between his father and Shimada. But he had never been very fond of his own father; neither could he remember being given any formal strictures concerning Shimada. "Who told you that?" he asked. "I don't think I did."

"Your brother told me."

He had thought as much; but in the end, it really did not matter what others had said. "I am not my father or my brother. As far as I am concerned, there isn't sufficient justification for refusing to see Shimada."

His wife could not know how very badly he wanted to avoid seeing the man again. She thought that her husband was simply being stubborn, and that in his perverse way was enjoying going against everybody else's wishes.

15

KENZŌ could remember clearly how as a child he used to trot along beside Shimada on their many outings together. Once he was taken to a seamstress to have a Western-style suit made. In those days, the Japanese had a very hazy notion of how Western adults, let alone children, dressed. The suit, when it was finished, was therefore a bizarre creation. The lapels of the jacket just managed to meet somewhere below his navel, where they were secured by two buttons. The jacket was made of pepper-and-salt cloth, extremely stiff and rough; the trousers were of coarse light brown twill, the kind of material favored by horse trainers. He was nevertheless very proud of his outfit.

His hat too was a great novelty to him. He delighted in the way the round felt object—it resembled a shallow cooking-pot upside down—fitted snugly over his close-cropped hair. It looked like—and indeed was—a skullcap. Once a conjurer in a vaudeville show that Shimada had taken him to see snatched away his precious hat and began playing tricks with it. In desperation he watched the conjurer push a finger through the shining black felt. When he got it back, he examined it closely to make sure that there really was no hole in it.

Shimada also bought him many of those goldfish with the beautiful long tails. And whenever Kenzō saw an illustrated children's book that he liked, Shimada would unhesitatingly buy it for him. Kenzō even possessed a miniature suit of knight's armor, authentic to the last detail, that fitted him perfectly. Hardly a day went by when he did not put it on and walk around the house shaking the toy baton made of gilt paper.

He was also allowed to play with a real sword small enough for a boy. The ornamental carving attached to the hilt depicted a mouse trying to drag a red pepper. The mouse was of silver and the pepper of coral. He regarded this piece of carving as his proudest possession. Often he tried to pull the blade out of the scabbard, but it was securely locked in. This fancy plaything from the days of the shogunate had been another token of Shimada's affection for him.

The two of them often went out boating, accompanied by a boatman dressed in the traditional straw skirt. When they were some distance from the land the boatman would cast his net, and Kenzō would watch the gray mullet with their silver scales dancing frantically as they were brought to the surface. Sometimes the boatman would take them three or four miles out and catch gilthead. On such occasions the boat rocked so much that Kenzō could hardly keep awake. He enjoyed himself most when a swellfish was caught. As it puffed up in anger Kenzō would tap it with a chopstick as though it were a drum.

Such childhood memories began to haunt him continually after his interview with Yoshida. They were fragmented but they were vivid nonetheless; and always Shimada figured in them. He realized, with surprise and pain, that so much of what he remembered was associated with the man.

But despite the clarity with which he could recall those childhood scenes, he was quite incapable of coloring them with any of the affection he might then have had for Shimada. His own lack of sentiment bothered him at first. Then gradually he began to wonder whether it was not simply because there had never really been any emotional bond between them.

Had Kenzō shared his memories with his wife, she might, in return for the chance to wallow in feminine sentimentality, have discarded some of her harsh thoughts about Shimada; but he kept them entirely to himself.

16

*A*T last came the uneasily awaited day. It was in the afternoon that Yoshida and Shimada arrived at Kenzō's house.

Kenzō was not quite sure how he should receive this man whom he had known so long ago. His intuitive social sense, which he would have relied upon under normal circumstances, now left him completely. They had not spoken to each other for twenty years, yet he felt no nostalgia whatsoever as he looked at the man sitting before him. He took no initiative in the conversation, and let the man do most of the talking; occasionally, he would reply in an almost offhand manner to some polite inquiry.

Shimada had a reputation for arrogance. Indeed, as far as Kenzō's brother and sister were concerned, Shimada's arrogance alone was enough reason for hating him. Kenzō, remembering this, began to feel defensive. I am not going to take any cheek, he said to himself, from the likes of him.

But Shimada was surprisingly polite. His speech was so proper that they might have been two strangers talking to each other for the first time. This man had once been used to calling Kenzō by his boyhood nickname of "Kenbō." Kenzō remembered how uncomfortable he had been when, even after their relationship had ended, this man had persisted in calling him "Kenbō."

So long as he continues to behave in this way, Kenzō thought, things will be all right. He tried his best to appear pleasant to his two guests. As for Shimada, it was obvious that in his anxiety not to annoy his host, he was doing his best to avoid references to the past; consequently, there was little they could talk about.

Kenzō thought of their recent encounter in the rain. "We met just the other day, didn't we?" he said. "Are you often in this neighborhood?"

"Yes. As a matter of fact, Takahashi's eldest daughter—she's married now—lives not too far from here."

Kenzō had no idea who Takahashi was. He said vaguely, "I see."

"You remember the Takahashis, don't you? They used to live in Shiba."

Kenzō thought he remembered having heard as a boy that Shimada's second wife had some relatives living there. Wasn't the head of that family some kind of priest? And wasn't there a son about his own age named Yōzō? Yōzō at least he had met a couple of times. "Let's see now," he said, "didn't your second wife's younger sister marry someone in Shiba?"

"No, no, it was her elder sister."

"Quite so."

"Her only son, Yōzō, died, but the girls have done very well for themselves. The eldest married someone you might have heard of." Shimada mentioned an author whose name was vaguely familiar to Kenzō. But this man, if Kenzō remembered correctly, was long since dead. "She's alone now, with a lot of small children to take care of. I'm the only man around, and they are always running up to their 'uncle' for help. They are having some repair work done on their house, and I've been asked to see that it's properly done. And so I pass by here almost every day."

Kenzō thought of that time when Shimada bought him a copy of Tung Ch'i-ch'ang's calligraphy manual at a secondhand bookshop in Ikenohata. Shimada never bought a thing without haggling over the price, and if after all the haggling he beat the price down even by a mere sen, he was pleased. At any rate, on that occasion, Shimada had bullied the poor bookseller into accepting somewhat less than he had initially asked for, then brazenly waited for his half-sen change. Kenzō had stood by with his book unhappily watching the ugly scene.

What must it be like, he wondered to himself, to be supervised by such a man? And as he imagined how angry the carpenters and the plasterers must be, he could not help smiling. Luckily, Shimada seemed not to notice the smile.

17

"THE family, mind you, isn't at all badly off. That book he wrote is still bringing in money, of course." Shimada seemed to assume that everybody would know what the book was. Kenzō had an idea that it was either a dictionary or some kind of textbook, but he was not interested enough to ask. "Writing is a wonderful business," Shimada continued. "You write one book and then sit back and wait for the money to come rolling in."

Kenzō refused to make a comment. There was an awkward pause in the conversation, and Yoshida started talking. When it came to making a profit, he said, no business could compare with writing books.

"After he died," Shimada said, "I decided that since I was the only man around I would have to take matters in hand. He had already received payment at the time the book came out, but I went to the publisher anyway and talked him into paying the family a certain amount in addition once every year."

"Well, think of that!" Yoshida said. "When you get down to it, a good education does pay off, doesn't it? These educated gentlemen, they really have an advantage over us."

"No doubt at all. It pays to have a good education, certainly."

Kenzō listened without interest. He knew he ought to take part in the conversation, but its nature was such that he could think of no appropriate remark to throw in. Bored and helpless, he looked at his two guests, then turned his gaze toward the garden.

It was a shabby garden, badly kept. The only decent-sized tree in it, a shapeless pine that looked as though it had never been trimmed, stood dejectedly by the fence. The needles were of a dull, almost black color. The ground had not been swept regularly, and was covered with stones.

"What about our professor here," he heard Yoshida saying. He turned and found Yoshida looking at him. "Why not turn out a book and make some money?"

Kenzō tried to smile. He had to be polite. "Yes indeed," he said, "a very good idea."

"He can dash off a book any time," Shimada said to Yoshida. "After all, he's studied abroad." His tone seemed to imply that he had made it possible for Kenzō to go abroad. Kenzō looked away in disgust. Shimada seemed quite unconcerned, however.

He would presumably have sat there for the rest of the afternoon if Yoshida had not at this point picked up his tobacco pouch and said to him, "It's getting late—perhaps we should be leaving."

Kenzō saw them off, then returned to the living room and sat down. It's as though he came simply to annoy me, he said to himself; is that what he wants? On the floor in front of him lay the cheap box of cookies Shimada had brought. Tiredly he gazed at it.

His wife came into the room to clear away the teacups and the ashtrays. She left him alone for a while, then came and stood over him. "Are you going to stay here?" "No," he said, standing up, "I'm going to the study." "Will those men come again?" "Probably," he said, and left the room.

From the study he could hear the sound of sweeping. This was followed by the cries of the children as they fought over the cookies. Then all was still. But again the silence was broken when rain began to fall from the twilight sky. He wondered how much longer he was going to put off buying himself a pair of over-shoes.

18

*A*FTER several days of rain the sun at last appeared. There was a touch of artificiality in the dark blue of the sky and the brilliant light. Kenzō's wife, who had whiled away the time sewing during the long depressing rain, now stepped out onto the verandah and looked up at the sky. Then she went quickly to her wardrobe and got out some clothes.

Kenzō was staring moodily at the shabby garden when he heard his wife come in. "What are you thinking about?" she said. He turned around and looked at her with tired eyes. She had put on her best clothes. How nice and fresh she looks, he thought. He was touched, and in a tone gentler than usual he said, "Are you going somewhere?" "Yes," she said. Her reply seemed to him much too curt. Once more he returned to his shell. "And the children?" "I'll take them with me. If I leave them here they're sure to annoy you."

When they came home Kenzō had already eaten his dinner and gone back to the study. It was quite dark outside. She looked in to tell him they were home. He thought it quite insensitive of her not to apologize for being late. He merely glanced at her in acknowledgment of her presence and said nothing. In disappointment and anger she left the room. He had lost his opportunity of asking her where she had been.

They found each other so unapproachable and uninteresting that conversation had become for them only a means of passing on essential information. They had long ceased to find pleasure in it.

At the dinner table two or three days later she at last made reference to her outing. "I went to see my parents the other day, and who do you think was at the house? My uncle from Moji! It was a shock, I can tell you. I had no idea he had come back from Taiwan."

This uncle from Moji was a black sheep. Once, when Kenzō and his wife were still living in the provinces, he had suddenly appeared at their house with a request for a loan. Kenzō, not knowing any better, got some money out of his savings account and lent it to him. A few days later a most impressive receipt arrived in the mail. In it the uncle had even stated the rate of interest he would pay. It all seemed unnecessarily formal to Kenzō at the time. But of course he never saw the money again.

"What is he doing these days?" he asked.

"I've no idea. He did say he was thinking of starting some kind of company, though. He wants to know what you think of the idea, and he's intending to come over to see you some time."

Kenzō thought he knew exactly what his wife's uncle had in mind. He was starting a new company the last time Kenzō saw him. Kenzō's father-in-law had been fooled too by the same story. Indeed, he had been dragged all the way to Moji and shown a building being put up. It was to house the company's offices, he was told. It never occurred to him that his brother-in-law might be showing him somebody else's building. His credulousness cost him several thousands.

Kenzō did not want to hear any more about the uncle, and his wife was only too willing to stop talking about him. But surprisingly enough she did not let the conversation die at this point. "It was such a fine day," she said, "that I decided to pay your brother a visit on the way back." Kenzō could not find anything untoward in that. After all, his brother did live quite near her parents.

19

IN an accusing tone she said, "Your brother was shocked when I told him that Shimada had been at our house. Shimada has no right to expect anything from you, he said, and you shouldn't be seeing him at all."

"You mean to say you went all the way to my brother's house just to hear that?"

"Why do you have to be so nasty? Why must you always be so suspicious of other people's motives? I went to see him simply because I thought it was high time one of us paid him a visit."

It was true that Kenzō himself hardly ever called on his brother. She was only trying to make up for her husband's negligence, he thought. He really had no right to complain.

"Your brother is worried for your sake," she continued. "He thinks that if you start seeing him again there's bound to be trouble."

"What kind of trouble does he have in mind?"

"Well, he's not likely to know until it happens, is he? I suppose all he means is that whatever happens, it's not going to be pleasant."

Kenzō hardly needed to be told that. He said, "But it wouldn't be right to refuse to see him."

"Why not? After all, wasn't he given money when your relationship with him was annulled?"

It was in the spring of his twenty-second year, Kenzō remembered, that his father had given Shimada money to cover the cost of having taken care of him as a child.

"Besides," his wife said, "hadn't you already been living with your parents for fourteen or fifteen years when your father paid off Shimada?" Kenzō had no idea at exactly what age he had gone to live with Shimada and at what age he had been returned to his parents. "According to your brother, you went to him when you were two and left him when you were eight."

"Is that so?" Kenzō began again to think of his own distant past, which seemed no more real to him now than some ancient dream. Childhood scenes ran through his mind one after the other. They were brilliantly clear and detailed, like colored illustrations seen through a magnifying glass, but he could not date them.

"It must be so. Your brother tells me the dates were clearly mentioned in the papers your father and Shimada exchanged." Kenzō had never seen any of the documents concerning the annulment of his adoption. "You must have seen them. You've obviously forgotten."

"I may have gone back to my parents when I was eight, but until the annulment I did continue to see Shimada off and on. It isn't as though my association with him was completely ended when I left his house." Kenzō saw his wife purse her lips, and for some reason he felt very lonely. He said, "It's no fun for me to have to see him, you know."

"Then why do you see him? It's all so pointless. And why do you suppose he wants to see you?"

"I really don't know. Surely he too must see that it's pointless."

"But your brother is certain that Shimada intends to squeeze money out of you. He says you'll have to watch out."

"As far as money is concerned, I was careful to point out right at the beginning that I had none, so I don't think there's any need to worry about that."

"But you can never be sure with people like that."

She had had from the beginning the feeling that Shimada was after money. Kenzō, who had sought comfort in the fact that he had clearly warned the man no money would be forthcoming, now began to share his wife's uneasiness.

20

HE could not entirely shake off the uneasiness as he worked, but he was so busy he was forced to ignore it. The rest of the month passed quickly without further word from Shimada.

On the last day of the month his wife came into the study and handed him the account book filled with untidily penciled notations. He was surprised. It was his custom to give his wife his salary at the beginning of each month and to leave the management of household finances completely in her hands. Never before had she invited him, with no prodding on his part, to examine in detail her accounting of the month's expenditures. She'll manage somehow, he was used to telling himself. Whenever he needed money, he would ask her for it. Sometimes his expenditure on books alone came to a quite considerable sum.

Yet she would always calmly give him whatever he asked for. This made him suspicious, and he would wonder whether she was not taking advantage of his lack of concern and becoming too carefree. Occasionally he would say to her, "Don't forget, you've got to account to me for every penny you spend." She would pull a face. She was of the opinion that no wife in the world could be as economical as herself. "All right," she would mutter, but when the end of the month came, she would not show him the account book. When he was in a good mood, he kept quiet, but when he was not, he would insist on being shown it. Not that it ever made much sense to him. Of course, with his wife to help him, he could see how the totals had been arrived at. But when it came to such questions as how much fish they had eaten or how much rice, and whether or not they had paid too much for such items, he was completely at a loss.

On this particular occasion, then, he handed the book back to his wife after a perfunctory examination and said, "Is anything the matter?"

"Well, we are rather short," she said, and went on to explain in detail how difficult it had been for her to make ends meet.

"I can't understand how you've managed to keep going all these months."

"You realize, don't you, that we never have any money to spare."

This even Kenzō knew. Toward the end of the previous month, some old friends had invited him to go on a day's outing with them. He had had to refuse, simply because he couldn't afford the two yen the trip was to have cost. He said, "I know that we don't have very much, but I'd have thought there was just enough to live on."

Reluctantly, his wife told him that she had been forced to pawn some of her clothes.

Kenzō remembered seeing often, as a boy, his brother and sister sneaking out of the house with packages containing their best clothes. They looked so furtive and ashamed, one would have thought they were doing something criminal. How hurt I was, he thought, to see them like that.

He felt more dejected than ever as he asked, "Did you go to the pawnshop yourself?" He himself had never been inside a pawnshop, and he found it hard to imagine his wife, who was far less accustomed to poverty than he, going into one.

"No," she said. "I asked someone else to handle it for me."

"Who?"

"The old lady at the Yamano house. She has an account at this pawnshop."

Kenzō was too ashamed to ask any more questions. The clothes she had pawned, she must have brought with her at the time of their marriage—they had not even been bought with his money.

21

HE made up his mind to work harder and earn more money. Not long afterward he returned home with some extra money in his pocket. He pulled out the envelope containing the bills and threw it down in front of his wife. She picked it up and looked at the back to see where it had come from. Neither of them said a word.

Her expression was blank. I could have shown pleasure, she thought, if only he had said something kind. Kenzō, on the other hand, resented her seeming indifference, and blamed her for his own silence. The money would help them satisfy their material needs. As a means of bringing warmth to their relationship, it was quite useless.

Kenzō's wife could not bear to think that the money had brought them so little pleasure. A couple of days later she showed him a length of cloth and said, "I thought I would make you a kimono. How do you like it?" She was smiling cheerfully.

Kenzō doubted her sincerity. She thinks she's being clever, he told himself; she's not going to fool me with her phony charm. Chilled by his attitude, she quickly left the room. As he watched her leave, he thought unhappily: I have been forced somehow or other to behave like this to my wife.

When he saw her again he said, "I am not as heartless as you think I am. I could be as warm and affectionate as the next fellow, but you make me bottle up all my natural feelings."

"That's not true! Why should I want to do a thing like that?"

"You are always doing it."

She looked at him bitterly. She had no idea what Kenzō was getting at. "Your nerves are in a bad way," she said. "I wish you would try to be a little more understanding."

Kenzō could not pay much attention to what she was saying; he was too busy being angry with himself for having become so callous, so different from what he used to be.

"No one is doing anything to you," she said. "If you are unhappy, you have only yourself to blame."

They were getting nowhere. Each thought the other pig-headed and unsympathetic, not worth talking to seriously, and each thought that it was up to the other to make amends.

For a man of his education the additional work that Kenzō had taken on to supplement his income was not at all difficult. But he begrudged the time and energy that the work demanded. He was morbidly fearful of wasting valuable time, of dying before he had done something worthwhile.

He was now so busy that it was always evening when he got home.

On this day, as on other days, he hurried home in the approaching darkness. He felt very tired. He opened the front door roughly, and his wife, on hearing the noise, came out to greet him. Immediately she said, "That man was here today." He guessed at once that she meant Shimada. Saying nothing he went into the morning room. She followed him in and helped him change into Japanese clothes.

22

HE was seated by the brazier smoking a cigarette when his wife brought in his dinner on a tray. She was preparing to serve him when he asked, "Did he come in?"

The suddenness of the question confused her for a moment. She looked up, and saw her husband tensely waiting for her to answer. Then she realized he was referring to Shimada. "Oh, you mean him. Well, since you were out. . . ." Her manner was defensive. She seemed to think that her not having asked Shimada in would anger Kenzō.

"You didn't ask him in?"

"No. I kept him in the front hall."

"What did he say?"

"He said he had been away on a trip. He apologized for not having dropped in sooner."

The "apology" sounded suspiciously like a sly joke. "Where

would a fellow like him travel to? He's not the type to have business connections in the provinces. Did he by any chance tell you where he went?"

"No, he didn't. There was no reason why he should. But he did say that his daughter had asked him to come. I take it he means that Onui person."

Kenzō had once met Shibano, the man whom Onui had married. And very recently, he had heard from Yoshida where Shibano was now stationed. It was at some brigade or divisional headquarters in a city in the midlands.

There was a long pause. Seeing that Kenzō was not about to say anything, his wife went on, "Her husband—he is a soldier, I believe."

"How is it you know so much?"

"Your brother once told me."

Shibano, Kenzō remembered, was a strongly built, dark skinned man. His features were rather fine, however, and Kenzō supposed that all in all he could be called a handsome fellow. Onui too was good-looking. She had a slim, graceful figure. She was fair skinned, and had an old-fashioned oval face. Her best feature perhaps was her eyes—long and slanting, with thick lashes. The two were married when Shibano was still a subaltern. Kenzō remembered visiting them at their new home right after their marriage. Shibano had just come home from the barracks and was sprawled out by the brazier. Beside him was a large glass of saké. He would reach for it from time to time and take a swig. Onui was powdering her face in front of a mirror. Her neck and shoulders were bare. Kenzō had sat idly by, hungrily eating his share of the sushi.

"Is Onui pretty?" his wife asked.

"Why do you want to know?"

"They tell me that for a while there was talk of you two getting married."

There had indeed been such talk. He was reminded of the time he had gone to pay the Shimadas a visit. He was about fifteen then, and he had a friend with him. As they approached the house they saw a girl standing on the little bridge in front of the gate. She smiled at Kenzō, and gave a little bow of welcome. Later the friend, who had just begun taking German lessons, had to have his childish fun. "So your *frau* always waits at the gate, eh?" he said.

Actually, Onui was a year older than Kenzō. Besides, Kenzō at the time could not even tell the difference between a pretty face and a plain one, nor could he decide whether he liked girls or not. True, he did experience a certain erotic sensation whenever he saw girls, and he was vaguely aware of his own desire to be near them; but this made him all the more antagonistic toward them.

At any rate, the suggestion that they should get married was far-fetched from the start and was quickly forgotten.

23

"*WHY* didn't you marry Onui?"

Kenzō, who had been staring at the dinner tray as though in a dream, quickly looked up. "It was all Shimada's idea. No one else took it seriously. And don't forget, I was only a child at the time."

"She isn't really that man's daughter, is she?"

"Of course not. Onui was Ofuji's child by her previous marriage." Ofuji was the name of Shimada's second wife.

"I wonder what kind of a life you would be leading now if you had married Onui."

"Since I didn't marry her, it would be impossible to say, wouldn't it?"

"You might have been happier, you know."

"I quite agree," he said impatiently. She became quiet. "There is no point in talking about these things," he added.

She did not have it in her to let the rebuke go unchallenged. "You never did care very much for me," she said.

Kenzō flung down the chopsticks and held his head. Angrily he began to scratch it, letting loose great quantities of dandruff.

He retired to his study. He was interrupted once when the children came in to say goodnight. When they left he went back to his reading. His wife sat in another room, trying to finish the sewing she had started that afternoon.

It was two days later that the subject of Onui came up again. This time too she was mentioned in a context that had no direct bearing on her. Kenzō's wife had come into the study with a postcard. She gave it to him, and instead of leaving immediately as she always did, sat down beside him. He absentmindedly held the postcard in his hand and kept on reading. She waited as long as she could, then said, "It's from Hida. It has to do with that man." Kenzō at last looked at the postcard. Hida wanted him to go over to his house and talk about Shimada. He would be at home on such and such a day, at such and such a time. He realized Kenzō was busy, and he hoped it would not be too inconvenient.

"What do you think he has in mind?" she asked.

"I don't know. But he isn't suggesting I have problems I want to discuss with him, surely?"

"Maybe they are going to advise you to have nothing more to do with Shimada. I see that your brother is going to be there too."

Kenzō looked at the postcard again. Onui's mother, Ofuji, had been no less anxious than Shimada to unite their family and Kenzō's through marriage. But whereas Shimada had wanted Kenzō to marry Onui, Ofuji had pinned her hopes on his brother. Kenzō remembered Ofuji saying to him, "It's too bad your family and ours aren't on speaking terms any more. Your people are the sort I'd like to be friendly with." That was a long time ago.

"But hadn't Onui been engaged to this soldier all along?" his wife asked.

"Yes. But I suppose both Shimada and Ofuji were quite prepared to break the engagement if one of us was willing."

"Whom would Onui have married if she'd had the choice?"

"How would I know?"

"And your brother—what did he want to do?"

"I don't know that either."

He really did not know. He had never been curious about the sentimental yearnings of those people that surrounded him in his childhood and youth.

24

H_E wrote a postcard to Hida saying he would come. And when the appointed day arrived, he set out for his brother-in-law's house in Yotsuya.

He was an extremely punctual man. In many ways he was inclined to be careless, unaware, but in certain matters he could be neurotically conscientious. On his way to Yotsuya he took out his watch twice. Every day, from morning to night, he felt as though he was being chased by time.

He thought about his work. It was not progressing at all satisfactorily. Every time he took one step forward toward the goal, it seemed to move one step further from him.

Then he thought about his wife. She had once suffered terribly from hysteria. It had gone away in time, but the possibility of its recurring haunted him.

And what about her parents? He was sure they were having money trouble. He began to feel like an inexperienced traveler waiting nervously for the next roll of the ship.

He had to think also of his sister and brother—and of course of Shimada. They all carried with them the stink of decay. And his life was tied to theirs by blood and a shared past.

He arrived at his sister's house in a state of mingled depression and nervous tension.

Hida came out to the hall to greet him. "It was very kind of you to come all this way," he said. His manner was ingratiating. How his attitude toward me has changed, Kenzō thought sadly; at least as far as my brother-in-law is concerned, I'm a success.

"I've been wanting to call on you," Hida said, "but I'm so terribly busy these days. I was on night duty last night, and they asked me to stay tonight too, but I had to tell them of course that I had business at home. I got back just a minute ago."

He was so convincing that Kenzō began to wonder whether there was any truth at all in the rumor that he had set up a mistress near his office. But, Kenzō had to remind himself, Hida was a man of very limited ability, and his services could not be quite so much in demand as he claimed.

As they sat down Kenzō asked, "And how is Onatsu?"

"Her asthma is giving her trouble again."

Kenzō got up and went to the adjoining room. He opened the door and looked in. His sister was seated in the middle of the room, wheezing noisily. At her side was her workbox, which she had made into an armrest by padding the top. Her hair was a mess. She was so ugly and pathetic Kenzō could hardly bear to look at her. "How are you?" he said. She did not have the strength even to turn her small, shriveled head around. She tried to say something, but the effort brought on a violent, protracted fit of coughing. He looked on helplessly, wondering how much longer it was going to last. "It must hurt," he said, half to himself.

A woman in her forties, unknown to Kenzō, was busily rubbing Onatsu's back. On a tray beside her was a cup of cold millet gruel. She looked up and gave Kenzō a little nod. "She's been like this since the day before yesterday," she said.

Every year his sister had an attack of this sort which lasted three or four days. During that time she would go without sleep or food. Then invariably she would begin to revive, and her naturally resilient body would be more or less fit again in a few days. Yet Kenzō was filled with uneasiness as he watched her. Her coughing had stopped temporarily, and she was now trying to breathe in short, loud gasps. "Don't try to talk, or you'll start coughing all over again," he said, and went back to Hida.

25

HIDA was nonchalantly reading a book. He brushed aside Kenzō's worried questions, saying, "Oh, she's all right—it's no worse than usual." The poor woman was wasting away before his very eyes, yet he was totally unconcerned. During the thirty years of their marriage, this man had not once said a kind word to his wife.

He put down his book and took off his steel-rimmed spectacles. "I was reading this while you were talking to her," he said. "It's not much of a book, I'm afraid."

Kenzō had somehow never associated Hida with reading. "What is it?" he asked.

"It's nothing you'd be interested in. It's one of those Edo-period frivolities."

With a grin Hida picked up the book and handed it to Kenzō. It was *The Tales of Jozan*. Why, Kenzō said to himself in surprise, this isn't at all a bad book. But good book or not, it was typical of this man to have been reading calmly while his wife was coughing her life out in the next room.

"I'm behind the times, I suppose," said Hida, "but I do like these old adventure tales." Obviously, he did not know the real literary worth of *The Tales of Jōzan*. On the other hand, he seemed vaguely aware that Yuasa Jōzan was not quite a hack,

"The fellow was something of a scholar, wasn't he? How would he compare with Bakin? Incidentally, I have Bakin's *Eight Dogs*."

Kenzō could see the handsome set—clearly a limited edition—standing neatly in the paulownia bookcase by the wall.

"Do you have *The Famous Sights of Edo*, Kenzō?"

"No, I don't."

"Now there's an interesting work. I'm very fond of it. I'll lend it to you, if you like. You can tell exactly what places like Nihonbashi and Sakurada looked like in those days."

This set was in a bookcase in the alcove. It was an old Mino-paper edition in pale blue binding. Hida picked out a couple of volumes and showed them to Kenzō. His manner seemed to suggest that Kenzō might never have even heard of *The Famous Sights of Edo*. Actually, Kenzō had come to know it very well as a child. He had spent many happy hours in the family storehouse staring at the illustrations. There was one that stood out most clearly in his mind now: it was entitled "Surugachō," and among the things depicted in it were the Echigoya shop front and Mt. Fuji.

How long was it, he asked himself, since he had last read a book for fun? He had lost not only the leisure of his childhood days but the capacity for enjoyment also. He looked at what he had become—a desperate, struggling creature—and for a moment was overcome by disappointment and self-pity.

His brother had still not appeared. Afraid perhaps that Kenzō might be getting impatient, Hida continued to chatter about books. He seemed strangely confident that this was the only way to keep Kenzō amused. Unfortunately, his knowledge of literature was slight. It was not at all surprising that he should have taken *The Tales of Jozan* to be merely a collection of adventure stories. Yet he owned a complete set, and an old one at that, of *The Famous Sights of Edo*.

Very soon he had exhausted the subject of books. To fill in the awkward silence he said, "Chōtarō ought to be here by now. He surely can't have forgotten—I reminded him often enough. Besides, he told me he had to get home by eleven at the latest. I think he was on the night shift last night. Should I send someone to fetch him?"

The quiet spell was over in the next room, and another long siege of coughing began.

26

AT last they heard someone coming into the house. "He's here, it seems," Hida said. But the footsteps went straight past their room. Then they heard a voice exclaiming, "Bad again? A pity. When did it start? I had no idea...." It was Chōtarō.

Hida was as usual impatient. "Hurry up, Chōtarō!" he called out. "We've waited for you long enough!" Who cares about her asthma, he might as well have said. But then, he was behaving exactly as anyone who knew him would have expected. His callousness was notorious.

"Yes, yes, all right, I'm coming!" Chōtarō sounded peeved. Obviously, he wasn't going to move; they heard him say to Onatsu, "Why don't you try eating some rice gruel? No? But you've got to eat something to keep going." Onatsu was trying to get her breath back, and she gave no reply. The woman whom Kenzō had seen rubbing her back said something appropriate instead. Chōtarō was a more frequent visitor at this house than Kenzō, and he seemed to know the woman quite well. The two now started chatting to each other.

Hida was in a sulk. Irritably he began to rub his dark skinned face with both hands, as if he had suddenly decided it needed a wash. He said in a low voice, "The trouble with that woman is she talks too much. If we had a maid, we wouldn't have to ask her to come and help us." He had been wanting to say something nasty, and had found a suitable victim.

"Who is she?" Kenzō asked.

"She works for the local hairdresser, remember? Her name is Osei. You must have seen her often when you used to come here in the old days."

"Really?" Kenzō had no recollection of having met the woman before.

"Of course you know Osei. She's a kind and honest woman, as you can see, but it really is too bad she's so garrulous. Talking is a disease with her."

Kenzō was skeptical. Hida was not averse to exaggeration when it suited his purpose.

Onatsu began coughing again, and even Hida became quiet. Chōtarō was still in the next room.

"It sounds worse than before," Kenzō said uneasily, and tried to get up. With a quick, impatient gesture Hida stopped him. "Don't worry," he said. "There really is nothing to worry about. It's only a chronic complaint, after all. It shocks you to see her like that because you haven't lived with it as I have. She gets these attacks all the time, you know. If I hadn't learned to ignore them, I couldn't have stood being married to her this long."

Kenzō did not know what to say. He remembered his own suffering when his wife had those hysterical fits, and could only marvel at Hida's indifference.

The coughing subsided, and at last Chōtarō appeared. "Sorry to be so late," he said. "I did mean to come earlier, but I had an unexpected guest, a fellow I hadn't seen for years."

"I was beginning to wonder if you were ever going to show your face," Hida said. "You're so late, it's not funny. We were about to send somebody over to fetch you." He was treating Chōtarō with excessive familiarity. No doubt he had reason to feel that he was entitled to do so.

27

THE three men immediately got down to business. Hida was the first to speak. He fancied himself a man of affairs, and became rather pompous at such times. In any session of this sort, however petty the problem being discussed, he had to be top man. Everybody laughed at him behind his back. "If he wants to be boss, let him—he can't do much harm."

"What do you think, Chōtarō?" he began.

"Well, let me see. . . ."

"The whole thing is so far-fetched, it seems hardly worthwhile telling Kenzō."

"Quite right. We certainly can't be expected to take a suggestion like that seriously at this late date."

"That's why I turned him down flat. 'Give up the idea,' I said to him. 'It's like killing one's child and then going to a priest years afterward and asking him if he can do anything to bring the child back to life.' But of course, his lordship wouldn't budge an inch. You know why he thinks he can come here as if he owned the place, don't you? Well, once I had to go to him about some trouble I was having with a girlfriend. But that was ages ago. Besides, I paid the money back to him with interest."

"That goes without saying," said Chōtarō. "When did he ever lend money without interest?"

"That's right. He's always saying that he thinks of us as his relatives, but when it comes to money, we'd be better off dealing with a total stranger. He's a real hard customer, that one."

"You should have told him all that when he was here."

Hida and Chōtarō seemed to have forgotten Kenzō's presence. Deciding he had let them go on long enough, Kenzō said, "What happened anyway? Did Shimada come here?"

"How stupid of me," Hida said. "I make you come all the way out here and then waste your time with senseless chitchat." He turned to Chōtarō. "Would you like me to tell Kenzō?"

"Yes indeed."

What Hida had to tell was unexpectedly simple. Shimada had called recently. He was getting old, he said, and didn't want to go on living all alone. Would Kenzō become his adopted son once more? And would Hida act as intermediary in the negotiation? It was an unbelievably barefaced proposal. Hida rejected it outright. But Shimada remained immovable, and finally Hida was forced to promise at least to relay Shimada's wish. That was all Hida had to tell.

Kenzō was nonplussed. "What an odd business," he said.

"It certainly is," Chōtarō said. "But then, he's got to the age when men begin to do odd things. He's over sixty, you know."

"He's become senile from greed," Hida said, and the two of them laughed.

Kenzō did not join in. He was too busy being puzzled by Shimada's proposal. There was nothing the man had said or done recently that would have led one to anticipate it. Had there been any suggestion of it when Yoshida first came to the house, or when Yoshida and Shimada came together, or when Shimada called in his absence? No, he concluded, he had been given absolutely no reason to foresee such an outcome. He said again, this time to himself, "What an odd business." Then pulling himself together he looked at the others and said, "It really isn't a serious problem. All we have to do is say no."

*A*S far as Kenzō was concerned, Shimada's request was so nonsensical it was hardly worth bothering about. Reject it outright and that should be the end of it.

"But," said Hida defensively, "I should have been shirking my duty had I not talked to you about it." He had called the meeting, and he wanted, it seemed, to justify himself. He was now entirely solemn. "Besides," he added, "remember the kind of man we are dealing with. There's no telling what he will do if we make the wrong move. We've got to be careful."

Chōtarō said chidingly, "Come now, you yourself just said he was senile. So why make all this fuss?"

"Don't you see, it's because he's senile that we must be careful. Had he been normal, I would have said no right then and there."

Finally, after a few more such irrelevant remarks, the long obvious conclusion was reached: Hida would contact Shimada and reject his proposal on Kenzō's behalf. The meeting had been rather a waste of time for Kenzō. Yet he was obliged to thank Hida. "Not at all," said Hida with self-satisfaction, "it's nothing." He looked to be settling down happily to a sociable evening. Looking at him now, no one would have thought that here was a man kept so busy at the office that he could rarely come home.

There were salt crackers in front of him, and he proceeded to eat these noisily. Many times he poured tea into a large bowl and gulped it down.

"Still a big eater, aren't you?" Kenzō said. "I suppose even now you can manage two servings of eel casserole?"

"Hardly. When you are fifty, you begin to slow down. Remember those days, Kenzō, when I thought nothing of going through five bowls of tempura and noodles?"

Hida's appetite in the old days had indeed been phenomenal. He used to be proud of it, and would always invite flattering comments about his large belly by slapping it ostentatiously.

Often, when Kenzō was a child, Hida would take him to a stall after a vaudeville show for a stand-up supper of tempura or sushi. Hida considered himself well versed in the ways of vaude-villians, and would try to teach Kenzō their argot and suchlike.

"When you get down to it," Hida was saying, "nothing beats eating on your feet. I've done a great deal of eating in all kinds of places in my time, as you know. Which reminds me, Kenzō, next time you go through Karuizawa, be sure to try the noodles there, just once. You eat it on the platform, you see, while the train is standing. It really is good—no wonder they call Karuizawa the home of buckwheat noodles."

Hida was an inveterate tourist, and had gone on pseudo-pilgrimages to temples all over the country. "You know what I once saw in the ground of Zenkōji temple, Chōtarō? An out-building with a large sign saying 'lessons given by the hereditary master of tōhachi.'* I was a little taken aback, I must say."

"You should have gone in for a lesson."

"And pay a fee? No thank you."

This is like the old days, Kenzō thought comfortably as he listened to the conversation. Yet he was very conscious too of how far apart these two were from him. Hida seemed not to notice Kenzō's aloofness. He said, "You've been in Kyoto, haven't you, Kenzō? Well, did you ever come across that curious bird they have over there that sings 'bring your plate, bring your plate, plenty to eat, plenty to eat'?"

He finally stopped talking when his wife began coughing painfully again. He brought his hands up to his dark face and rubbed it irritably.

Chōtarō and Kenzō got up and went into the next room. They sat by their sister's bed until the coughing was over, then left the house and separately went home.

29

*H*E was once more involved in a world which for a while had become merely a part of the past. He had always known, of course, that some day this world would force itself on him, that his own present life would become entangled again with the lives of those who had never left it. There was Hida, who with his rough-cropped head reminded him so much of a mendicant priest; there was his sister, struggling for breath like some cat dying in a shadowy place, and his brother, with his exhausted, dried-up face.

Long ago, he had been one of them, but circumstances had removed him from them and his native city. It was with some

---

* A variation of the children's game, "paper, scissors, rock."

sense of nostalgia that he had returned after a long absence, but this nostalgia was overshadowed by too many distasteful memories.

He made himself think of that part of his present existence which had nothing to do with these people. In his mind he now saw youthful faces, eager and bright-eyed. He could hear the young men laughing, as though in anticipation of future happiness, and for a moment his depression lifted.

One day shortly after the meeting at Hida's house, Kenzō and one of the young men went for a walk to Ikenohata. On the way home, as they were walking along a street which branched off the main road, they came upon a newly built geisha exchange. Kenzō looked quickly at his young companion. He was reminded, he said, of a story he had heard concerning a certain woman. This woman, when still a young geisha, had committed murder, and after twenty miserable years in prison had recently been released. What could such a woman look forward to now, he wondered. What would she do, without her youth and good looks? "How wretched and lonely she must be," he said. His companion, however, seemed quite indifferent. For him, it would always be spring. Kenzō saw the gulf between himself and this young man of twenty-three, and was shocked.

He thought of his own condition, and asked himself, "Am I really very different from her?"

It seemed to him that the grey in his hair had of late become more conspicuous than ever. Ten years had passed him by, leaving him with a sense of time lost and things unaccomplished.

"I can't help identifying myself with her," he said. "The fact is, I spent all of my youth in prison too." The young man looked at him in surprise. "I am talking about college. And the library. In their own way they are prisons." The young man said nothing. Kenzō continued: "But what else could I have done? Without those years of imprisonment, I wouldn't be what I am now." He seemed to be deriding himself, yet apologizing.

The lonely years he had spent thus far had been a necessary preparation for the present, he told himself. And whatever he was going through now was a necessary preparation for the future. What he had done and what he was doing was right. Yet sometimes he could not avoid the thought that his life amounted to little more than simply growing old.

"Study all your life, then die—it's all rather pointless," he said.

"Of course not," said the young man. He had not, after all, understood Kenzō.

Kenzō wondered, as he walked, what changes his wife must see in him since the time of their marriage. She herself aged noticeably each time she had a child. At times she would lose so much hair that one felt her very life was ebbing out of her. And now she was in her third pregnancy.

30

WHEN he returned home he found his wife napping in the living room. Beside her were a sewing box and bits of cloth. He pulled a face at the untidy scene, as if to say, "What, again?"

His wife liked to sleep. On some mornings she got up after he did, and there were even times when she would go back to bed after seeing him off to work. Her usual excuse was that unless she had plenty of sleep she felt so dull she hardly knew what she was doing. Kenzō was not sure whether he should believe her or not. He was inclined to be skeptical particularly when, after he had chided her about her habit, she would promptly slip back into it without any apparent shame. "You're doing it just to spite me," he would say. He knew that in view of her tendency to hysteria he should not be too critical, but the thought that her uncouth habit might spring from mere perverseness often angered him.

She would stay up until all hours of the night. "Why don't you go to bed at a reasonable hour?" he would say. "Because I have insomnia," she would invariably answer, and continue her sewing.

He hated her for what he took to be her perverseness and incorrigibility. At the same time he feared her hysteria, and the possibility that his explanation of her conduct might be mistaken made him deeply uneasy.

She was lying on her side, with her head resting on her arm. He remained standing, and stared for a while in silence at her pale profile. He made not the slightest effort to wake her.

He then caught sight of a bundle of papers beside her bare white arm. They seemed to be neither letters not printed matter.

They were brown with age, and tied together neatly with old-fashioned paper cord. Half hidden under her loose hair, they looked, from where he stood, as if they were being used for a pillow.

He was not curious enough to pick them up. He turned his gaze again to his wife's pale face. Her cheek formed a deep, angular hollow in her profile. A woman relative of hers, whom she had not seen for a long time, had recently called on her. On first seeing her the relative had cried out appalled, "How thin you've become!" Kenzō at the time had somehow felt that he alone was to blame.

He now went into his study. Half an hour later he heard his children come home. They were arguing loudly with the maid. Then he heard them going into the living room. "Be quiet!" his wife shouted.

A few minutes later she appeared in the study, holding the papers. "Your brother called while you were out," she said.

Kenzō stopped writing. "Is he gone?"

"Yes. I told him you had gone out for a walk and that you should be coming home soon. But he said he was in a hurry and couldn't stay. He was on his way to a friend's funeral. He was afraid he might be too late as it was. He hoped you wouldn't go out again, since he would try to drop in on his way home."

"What did he want to see me about?"

"It's apparently about that man again," she said. She meant Shimada.

31

S*HE* handed the papers to him. "He asked me to give these to you."

Suspiciously he said, "What are they?"

"They are concerned with that man, I think. Your brother said that he decided to get them out today and bring them over since they might be of some use to you."

"I never knew they existed."

Vaguely, without much interest, he glanced at the musty, worm-eaten papers in his hand. They must have been kept in some damp, airless place, he thought. As he passed his finger over the irregular line of holes the worms had made, his eyes seemed briefly to gaze into the past, but he was really in no mood to undo the neat knot and start examining them one by one.

He said, "What good will it do to look at these things now?"

"Your father put them away carefully for future reference."

"Quite so." He did not share his wife's seeming respect for his father's good sense in such matters. "Knowing him, I should say it's more than likely that he hoarded these things simply for the sake of hoarding them."

"Surely he did it out of consideration for you. He told your brother to keep them carefully since you could never tell what a fellow like that might do."

"Is that so."

His father had died of a stroke. Kenzō was not present at his death, having left Tokyo long before. It was therefore not at all strange that the papers should have been in Chōtarō's keeping all this time without his knowledge.

At last he untied the cord and began separating the various papers. One set clearly pertained to agreements reached between his father and Shimada. There was one paper entitled "Acknowledgment of receipt of payment for January, 1888." At the bottom were Shimada's seal mark and, in his handwriting, the words "above month's installment duly received."

"It appears that my father had to pay out three or four yen a month."

"To that man?" His wife was craning her neck in an attempt to read the document.

"I wonder," Kenzō said, "how much my father gave him altogether. I have an idea he once gave him a lump sum besides these monthly payments. And it's not like him not to have kept the receipt. It must be here somewhere."

Cursorily he looked through the papers. But there were so many of them, and they looked so much alike, that he gave up the search. Finally he picked up a packet of fairly thick papers folded in four. "Why," he said, "these are my primary school diplomas." One could tell from these that the school had changed its name a few times during the period of his attendance. The name printed on the oldest of the diplomas was "Primary School No. 8, Fifth Middle School District, First University District."

"What was the diploma for?" she asked.

"I forget."

"It looks very old."

There were some certificates of merit. On each was an imposing seal mark—a circle formed by two dragons—with the class of honors shown in the middle. The prize described on all of them was writing brush and paper. He said, "I know I was given a book sometimes."

He would rush home from the ceremony joyfully clutching some textbook on ethics or world geography. And during the night before, he would lie awake wondering whether he would win a prize or not. To Kenzō now, those days seemed far less distant than they once did.

32

HIS wife picked up the diplomas he had put down and began to read each one. She obviously found them very intriguing.

"'Sixth grade, lower primary school'—how odd it sounds."

"Well, they had such things in those days."

He proceeded to go through the remaining papers. He found his father's handwriting almost illegible. "Look," he said, "how can I make sense out of something like this? The handwriting is impossible to begin with, and then there are all these corrections...."

It was the first draft of a letter from his father to Shimada. He gave it to his wife. With the meticulousness typical of women she managed to decipher the writing.

"Did you know that once your father looked after Shimada?"

"I did hear something of the sort."

"It says so here: 'In consideration of the fact that the said person, when a child and thus unable to earn a living, was for five years given shelter in our house....'"

To Kenzō's ears it sounded like one of those Tokugawa-period petitions. What an old-fashioned man he was, he thought. He remembered how his father would sit him down and describe, in a language appropriately respectful, the hawking expeditions of the Shogun. But of course his wife was interested merely in the content, and was quite blind to the stylistic peculiarities. "So that's the connection," she said. "Shimada was adopting a son of his old benefactor. Look, later on it says so quite explicitly."

Kenzō was filled with pity for his own unfortunate childhood. Unaware of how her husband felt, she went on gaily: "'Consequently Kenzō, then two years of age, was duly adopted. However, in view of the long-standing disharmony between the said person and his wife, Tsune, and their subsequent divorce, Kenzō, being at the time eight years of age, was returned to us. From that time to the present, namely for a period of fourteen years, Kenzō has been under our care. . . .' Really, it's so messy I can't make the rest out."

She squinted hard at the writing, while Kenzō sat by patiently. Then she began to giggle. "What's so funny?" he said. She turned the manuscript around so that he could see it, and pointed her finger at a line. It was an insertion minutely written in red ink. Slowly, and frowning with effort, he read out: "'The said person, having become familiar with a certain widow by the name of Tōyama Fuji. . . .'" He stopped and said, "This gets sillier and sillier."

"But it's true, isn't it?"

"Yes, I suppose so."

"So that's why you went back to your parents when you were eight."

"But the trouble was, Shimada wouldn't agree to make it formal. He wouldn't let me take back my original name."

His wife returned to the manuscript. She hoped that all the undecipherable passages notwithstanding, she would pick up something she didn't know. Toward the end she found a statement to the effect that Shimada had not only refused to make formal Kenzō's return to his family, but had secretly appointed him head of his own household, and had then gone around borrowing money under Kenzō's name.

The next paper they looked at was Shimada's receipt—again written in outlandishly formal language—for the money he received when he finally relinquished all rights to Kenzō. There it was clearly stated that he was given a lump sum to begin with, and would be given a specified sum every month for a period thereafter. All of this was to compensate him for the expense he had incurred in keeping Kenzō for five years.

"Why did they all have to be so wordy?" Kenzō said.

"Hida's name is down here as witness and go-between. I wonder if he actually wrote this?"

Remembering Hida's knowing air at their recent encounter, Kenzō thought it quite likely.

33

CHŌTARŌ did not show up that evening after all. "The funeral probably ended late," she said, "and he must have gone straight home."

He was not sorry. His job demanded constant preparation at home for the following day's assignment. It was inconvenient to say the least to have his precious time taken up by social visits of one kind or another. He put the cord around the papers, and as he pulled it tight it broke.

"It's obviously too old to be any good," she said.

"Hardly."

"The papers are all worm-eaten, so why shouldn't the cord be in the same condition?"

"Perhaps you're right. I suppose they were left discarded in some musty corner all these years. But you know, it isn't quite like my brother to have kept them. He's the sort that sells anything he can lay his hands on."

She looked at Kenzō, then began to laugh. "Who in the world would want to buy those things?"

"What I mean is, it's a wonder he didn't throw them into the waste basket, since he couldn't sell them."

She brought out some red-and-white string from the drawer in the brazier and secured the papers. "Here you are," she said. He looked hopelessly at the piles of books around him. "Where am I going to put them?" His strongbox was packed tight with old letters and notes. The only place with any room left was the cupboard where his bedding was put away during the day.

With a wry smile she stood up. "By the way, your brother will be paying us a visit in the next two or three days, I'm sure."

"To talk about the usual thing, I suppose."

"Probably. But he will have to bring back your hakama* anyway. He had to wear one to the funeral, so he dropped in to borrow yours."

Kenzō was reminded of the occasion of his own graduation from college. Then, it was he who had had to borrow his brother's clothes. He had gone with his friends afterward to have a picture taken at a photographer's in Ikenohata, wearing a limp, worn-out haori† his brother had given him. True, it was of silk and

---

* A kind of skirt worn by men on formal occasions.
† A loose black coat usually worn over the hakama.

had the family crest proudly printed on it, but anyone could tell that it was just managing to stay in one piece. He remembered one of the friends saying, "Which one of us will be the first to own a carriage?" Without replying Kenzō had looked sadly at his own haori. On another occasion, a good friend had invited him to a wedding reception at a rather formal establishment in Hoshigaoka. That time, he had had to borrow both hakama and haori from his brother. But such memories his wife could not share.

That he the borrower had now become the lender gave him no sense of accomplishment whatsoever; rather, it saddened him. "The fickleness of fortune"—trite as the phrase was, it seemed to have meaning for him at the moment.

"It's hard to believe," he said, "that he has no hakama even."

"I suppose in the course of all these years he has somehow lost everything."

"It's a bit awkward."

"Why? So long as we have the hakama, we might as well lend it to him. It isn't as though he wants it every day."

"Of course. But what happens if he comes to borrow it again and we haven't got it?"

He was thinking of his recent discovery that his wife had secretly been pawning her clothes. He was in a pessimistic mood, and he thought it not at all unlikely that he should soon be no better off than his brother.

In the old days he had always managed to stay independent no matter how poor. No one had looked to him for support, and he in turn had not depended on anyone. He was now as poor as ever, but this he did not mind so much. What was unbearable was that he, of all people, should be regarded by those around him as the only one that had done well for himself—as the only source, one might say, of their own vitality.

34

CHŌTARŌ was a lowly civil servant and worked in a large government office in the middle of Tokyo. That he should have pursued his pathetically insignificant career for so long in this magnificent building seemed to him incongruous. "There are plenty of young, eager fellows around," he would say. "Who has any use for a decrepit character like me?"

Several hundred men worked like slaves night and day in the building. His own energy was about to run out, and like a shapeless shadow in the midst of all the furious activity, he somehow managed to drag out his existence. By nature inclined to indolence, he secretly hated to work. He was sickly, and already he was dried up like an old man. Every morning he would leave for his office, his face drawn and without color, as though he were going to his death. "Having to stay up so many nights is ruining me," he would say. He caught cold easily and was always coughing. Sometimes he would feel feverish; and he would be frightened, thinking that perhaps he had tuberculosis.

The sort of work he did would have been hard even on a vigorous young man. Every other day he was put on night duty. After having worked through the night he would stagger home in the morning almost unconscious. All that day he would lie exhausted in bed, without the will to do anything. But he made himself go on, so that he and his family could survive.

"I really may lose my job this time," he would say whenever there was talk of a shake-up in the government. "Won't you speak to someone?" When Kenzō was living in the provinces, he had on more than one occasion been embarrassed by a letter from his brother asking him to intercede. The letter would contain a list of important government officials Kenzō might contact. But these were invariably mere names to Kenzō, hardly the kind of people he could write to about his brother's job.

Despite the crises, then, Chōtarō had hung on to his job. But in all the years of his service, he was never promoted. He was simply a piece of machinery installed in a corner of the office; it would tick away until it wore out. Sometimes Kenzō would look at this man, seven years his senior, and uncharitably think to himself, "Surely, in the twenty-five years he's worked there, he might have done something that attracted attention."

In his youth, the man had been quite different. He had been a rather gay type. He had no time for books, and would spend his time learning to play some musical instrument or other, or cooking a dish that momentarily caught his fancy. That he had been a wastrel in his youth, he was wont to admit to others: "You might say I am paying for my sins now."

Through the death of older sons, he became the heir. When their father died, he immediately sold the family property and with the proceeds paid off his old debts. He then moved into a small house. The contents of the old house that he couldn't get in there, he sold also.

Eventually he became the father of three children. The eldest daughter was his favorite. In her adolescence this girl became seriously ill with tuberculosis. He did everything in his power to save her, but to no avail. When after two years of illness she died, everything he owned was gone. In his wardrobe, there was not one respectable item of clothing left. The carefully tended suit that he now wore to the office was one that Kenzō had worn constantly while abroad.

35

*H*E came to the house again three days later, just as Kenzō's wife had predicted. He took the hakama out of the cloth wrapper and said to her, "Thank you. I'm sorry I kept it for so long." The hakama was meticulously folded—the sides over the waist stiffening. In the old days he had been terribly vain about his appearance, and would not have been seen carrying a parcel. The vanity was gone, and so was his vitality. As she watched him fussily refolding the wrapper, she noticed how dry-looking his hands were.

"This is a pretty good hakama," he said. "Did Kenzō have it made recently?"

"Oh no. Where would we find the money for that sort of thing? No, he's had it for a very long time." Her husband had worn it at their wedding. How solemn he looked then, she thought. The wedding had been an extremely simple affair, and had taken place in the provinces. Chōtarō had not attended it.

"Is that so? Come to think of it, I believe I've seen it before. They made things well in the old days, didn't they? It looks as good as new."

"That's because he hardly ever wears it. He must have had it made while still a bachelor. What possessed him, I can't imagine—it's so out of character."

"Perhaps he got it specially for the wedding."

Laughingly they talked about the strange ceremony. Her father had taken her all the way from Tokyo to the provincial town where Kenzō was then living. He had seen to it that his daughter would be appropriately dressed for the occasion; but for some reason he himself had come badly prepared, and attended the wedding in what was hardly more than lounging clothes. His manner too was rather informal: he sat through most of the ceremony cross-legged.

Poor Kenzō had only his old housekeeper to consult about the wedding. He was totally ignorant about such matters. As it had been originally understood that it should take place in Tokyo, even the go-between was not on hand to give him advice. True, this go-between had gone to great trouble to write out a set of instructions for Kenzō's benefit. But they helped very little. Written in very formal style, full of examples drawn from feudal manuals on etiquette, they were hardly designed for practical use.

"Needless to say, no one thought of having the proper decorations around. Why, even our nuptial cup was chipped."

"Do you mean to say," Chōtarō said, "that you used a chipped cup for the ceremony?"

"Yes, we did. That's probably why our marriage hasn't been exactly harmonious."

He looked understanding. "Kenzō can be pretty difficult."

She merely smiled. She did not seem to take her brother-in-law's remark very seriously. "He ought to be back by now," she said.

"I really must see him today, and talk to him about that business."

He was about to say more when she suddenly got up and went to the next room to look at the clock. When she came back she had the papers in her hand. "You would want these with you when you talk to him, I suppose?"

"I doubt it. I brought those along just so that Kenzō could look at them. You have shown them to him, haven't you?"

"Yes."

"What did he say?"

Evasively she said, "There are all kinds of papers here, aren't there?"

"Father went to a lot of trouble to keep those. They might prove essential, he said."

That she had read out to her husband a passage from what seemed the most significant of the papers she did not say. Chōtarō said no more about them. The two talked idly until Kenzō returned half an hour later.

36

KENZŌ changed his clothes as usual before joining the others. Chōtarō had the bundle on his lap and was trying to untie the string with his parched, old man's fingers. When he saw Kenzō, he began to tie it up again. "Hullo," he said. "I was just taking a peek at these. A lot of them, I see, don't concern you at all."

"I didn't know." Kenzō realized that his brother, despite the importance he seemed to attach to the papers, had not looked at them for a long time. That Kenzō himself had not examined them with much care was also clear.

Chōtarō said, "My request for permission to marry Oyoshi is in here, did you know?" He was referring to the formal application he had had to send to the ward office. They were both surprised that such a document should have been in the bundle.

Chōtarō had divorced his first wife. His second wife had died. When she was ill, he showed little concern and was hardly ever home. True, she was pregnant at the time, and at first she seemed to be suffering from nothing more than the usual bout of morning sickness. But even when she got much worse he remained callous, and people began to say that he had always disliked this wife who had been forced on him and was now having his revenge. Kenzō for one believed this.

He chose his third wife himself, after having received permission from his father. But he did not speak to Kenzō about his proposed marriage. Kenzō, vain as he was, resented this oversight, and began to direct his resentment even at the innocent prospective sister-in-law. He tormented his weak brother by insisting that he would not accept as sister-in-law an uneducated woman of such low station. "What an unrelenting, prejudiced man," people began to say of him behind his back. But when such comments reached his ears, he became even more insistent. He, the educated member of the family, was being the most conventional, but always apt to regard his own irrationality as some kind of intellectual virtue, he had then been blind to the irony of his position.

He now looked back with shame on his conduct at the time. He said, "Surely, you should keep the application."

"No, I don't need it. It's only a copy."

Kenzō found himself wondering when Chōtarō had married the woman. "When was it that you formally applied to the ward office?"

"Oh, it was a long time ago." A faint shadow of a smile appeared on his face. After two unsuccessful marriages he had at last been able to marry a woman of his own choosing, and he was not so decrepit as to forget the date of such an occasion. But he was not so young as to want to talk about it.

"How old is she?" Kenzō's wife asked.

"Oyoshi? Well, if I remember rightly, there's only a year's difference between you and her."

"She's still young then."

He gave no reply. He looked quickly at the papers which still lay on his lap and began to untie the string. "Look, here's another that has nothing to do with you. I was really quite surprised to find it here." Casually he pulled an old paper out of the now untidy pile. It was the first draft of his eldest daughter's birth register. Her name had been Kiyoko. "We hereby report the birth," it said, "of the above child at fifty minutes past eleven o'clock on the morning of the twenty-third day of this month." For some reason a line had been drawn in ink through the date. This line was crossed by another, more irregular, line of worm-holes. "This is in father's hand too," he said. With great care he turned the old scrap of paper around to show Kenzō. "It's worm-eaten, see? But that's not surprising, really. After all, this concerns someone who's already dead." He stared at the date of birth of the dead girl, and quietly repeated it to himself.

37

*H*AVING nothing to look forward to, Chōtarō had come to immerse himself completely in the past. And Kenzō could not help feeling that he too was being dragged back, that he was being taken further and further away from the life he wanted to lead. He pitied his brother's loneliness. But he was too preoccupied with his own future to offer more than pity. His own loneliness, indeed the prospect of continued loneliness in the years to come, he had long ago learned to accept as inevitable.

Chōtarō told him that Shimada's proposal had been duly rejected. But when asked in what manner Shimada had been informed of their decision, or what his response had been, he was at a loss. "Well, anyway, Hida said he took care of it, so that's that." Kenzō could not find out whether Hida had actually gone to see Shimada or had merely written to him.

"I should imagine he saw him," Chōtarō said. "On the other hand, Hida being what he is, he might simply have written a letter. I'm afraid I forgot to ask. Some time after our meeting I went back to see how Onatsu was. As usual Hida wasn't around. According to her at that time he hadn't done anything about getting in touch with Shimada—too busy apparently. You know how irresponsible he is. It's quite possible he wrote a letter and left it at that."

Kenzō too knew Hida to be irresponsible. But he was also the kind that liked to be asked to do things. And he would do what he was asked—provided that he was asked with the proper amount of humility and flattery.

Chōtarō seemed to feel that they were under some sort of obligation to communicate their decision to Shimada in person. "We have to remember," he said, "that Shimada took the trouble to go and see Hida." But despite his strict notions of propriety, he was always careful to maintain a passive role in such affairs. If some complicated problem arose that needed attention, he would automatically look away. And in his long-suffering fashion he would wait for it to solve itself. This foolish streak in him neither irritated nor amused Kenzō; rather, it made him sorry for him. It did occur to him that he might actually share this characteristic with his brother, and that therefore he was perhaps being sorry for himself.

He tried to change the subject. "And is Onatsu feeling better?"

"Yes, I think so. Asthma is a strange thing. Looking at her now, you would never think she could have been so ill."

"Can she talk?"

"Are you joking? You know what she's like—talk, talk, talk. By the way, she thinks Shimada got the idea from his step-daughter."

"I doubt it. Why not simply say that he has always been unreasonable? That makes more sense."

"True enough."

Kenzō could not hide his impatience when he saw that Chōtarō was giving the matter some serious thought.

"The other possibility, she said, is that he's become unwanted in his old age." Kenzō said nothing and let Chōtarō go on. "At any rate, he must be lonely. Mind you, it's because he misses money, not people." He had picked up the information somewhere that Shimada's wife, Ofuji, received a regular monthly allowance from her daughter. "Apparently she gets a portion of the extra pay that her son-in-law got with his military decoration. And this would of course make Shimada feel unbearably dejected. There's no limit to that fellow's greed."

Kenzō listened impassively. He could not summon up much sympathy for a man who was lonely for money.

38

SOME days passed without incident. This meant for Kenzō that they were spent in silence.

During this period he could not at times avoid losing himself in reminiscence. Like his brother, whom he pitied, he had become a man of the past.

He tried to cut his life in two, the past and the present. Yet the past refused to be sliced off, and was with him constantly. His eyes were focused on the future, yet his legs took him in the opposite direction.

Once his memory carried him down a trail at the end of which stood a large, square house. In it were wide stairs that led to the second story. The upstairs and downstairs seemed to his eyes exactly the same. The inner garden, surrounded on four sides by verandahs, was a perfect square.

Strangely enough, no one lived in this house. He was too young to feel lonely, to know that a house should be any different.

The house was to him like a town with a ceiling, and like a boy playing alone in deserted streets, he would run about the numerous adjoining rooms and the long, straight corridors. Sometimes he would go upstairs and look down on the road outside through the narrow latticework. He could see horses with bells and stomachers on them sauntering past. Right across the road a large bronze buddha sat cross-legged on a lotus. He held a staff and wore a broad-brimmed hat.

From the dark front entrance with its earthen floor he would cross the road where the horses passed and go down the stone steps to the buddha. Holding on to the staff Kenzō would stand on the trailing bottom folds of the ample cloak. He would edge his way around to the back and try to pull himself up onto the shoulders, but always the brim of the hat stopped him.

Near the square house and the buddha was a house with a red gate. It stood at the end of a winding lane, perhaps fifty yards from the road. The house was surrounded by a thick grove.

If one turned left at the end of the road one found oneself standing on the top of a long slope. There were stone-paved steps all the way down. Perhaps they were old, for the paving was extremely uneven. From between the stones long grass grew, and swayed in the wind. But these steps must have been regularly used. He, at any rate, went up and down them many many times.

The slope formed one side of a small valley. On the top of the slope opposite stood a grove of cedars, menacingly dark. At the bottom stood a thatched cottage that leaned slightly backward and to the right. From certain primitive touches that had been added to the front, one could tell that it was trying to be a tea-house. There were always, Kenzō remembered, two or three stools neatly arranged outside.

Once he peeked through the reed fence at the back of the cottage and saw a pond with rocks around it. A wisteria trellis stretched over the water at one end, supported by two posts sunk into the bottom. Azaleas grew in abundance around the pond; and occasionally one caught a glimpse of a patch of red moving about like a specter in the muddy water.

Kenzō felt he must try to catch the carp. He made himself a crude fishing pole, and one day, when there seemed to be no one in the cottage, he crept into the garden. He threw in the bait, and almost immediately the carp was pulling at it. As he felt the strain in his arms, he was suddenly afraid. The mysterious, powerful creature, he knew, was trying to drag him into the water. Throwing the pole down, he rushed away. He went back the next day and saw the carp, now quite still, floating on the surface. It was an eerie sight.

Kenzō could not remember who was looking after him then. But judging by the awareness of the boy in those scenes, he must have already begun living with the Shimadas.

39

PICTURES of the lonely countryside faded away, and now he saw vaguely a small house with a lattice window in the front. It had no outer gate, and stood in a narrow back street which curved away sharply on either side of it.

The house was always dark inside—the sun somehow seemed never to touch it—and it was perhaps fitting that his memory of it should be shadowy too.

He got smallpox while he was there. When he was older, he was told that it had been brought about by vaccination. He had rolled about screaming in his dark room, driven mad by the itching.

The house disappeared from his vision and was replaced by a large building. The floor seemed to be divided into partitions, but these seemed together to form one vast room. There were people dotted about here and there. But much of the floor was empty, and the expanse of the yellow straw matting gave the place the look of a deserted temple hall. He was eating his lunch on some high place. Accidentally he dropped whatever it was that he was eating—it was some kind of a roll made of fried bean curd—to the floor below. Many times he leaned over the railing, hoping that someone would pick it up. The adults he was with paid no attention, and continued to stare at the other end of the hall. There he could see a large house. Its walls began to quake, then it collapsed in a heap, and from an opening in the roof a splendidly mustachioed warrior emerged. Kenzō at the time had no idea he was watching a play.

For some unaccountable reason the play was associated in his mind with a hawk in flight. It had swooped past toward the green bamboo grove in the distance and someone beside him had shouted, "There it goes!" Then someone clapped his hands, trying to get the hawk to come back.

Which had come first—the hawk or the play, the countryside with the fields and groves or the dark house facing the mean city street—he did not know. And no one he knew seemed to figure in any of the scenes.

Not long after, the Shimadas had entered his awareness as his parents. They were living in an odd house in those days. The main entrance was at one end of the house. You turned right when you came out, and went up three stone steps beside the wall of another house. You were in a small alley, about three feet wide, which opened into a wide, busy street. In the house and to the left of the main entrance stretched a long verandah. Around the corner at the end of it there was a short flight of stairs that led down to a rectangular reception room. Alongside the room was an inner courtyard, also rectangular. There was another entrance on that side of the house, and you crossed the courtyard to get to it. Outside you looked onto a large river full of boats with white sails. On the bank were bundles of firewood piled up high behind stockades, and you walked down the gently sloping paths between these stockades to the water's edge. As you came to the stone embankment, crabs hiding in the gaps would stick out their claws.

The long house had once belonged to a merchant. Later it was split up into three apartments, and the Shimadas lived in the middle one. Who the merchant was, or why he had left the house, Kenzō did not know. The large reception room, where the merchant must have conducted his business, was for a time rented to a Westerner who gave English lessons. Westerners were still rather exotic creatures in those days, and Shimada's wife, Otsune, seemed to feel that she was living next to some kind of monster. This man would often saunter down the verandah in his slippers and stop outside the Shimada apartment for a chat. And whenever he saw Otsune lying in bed with her face all taut and pale—she was prone to nervous fits—he would make sympathetic noises in an incomprehensible mixture of English and Japanese with sign language thrown in.

40

BY the time young Kenzō realized that the Westerner had disappeared, the large room had already been turned into what today would be called the ward office.

Several clerks worked at their low desks arranged in a row. Western-style desks were not yet popular, and the clerks presumably did not mind sitting on the floor all day long. Townsmen who had either been called there or come of their own accord would take off their clogs in the courtyard, and each would go deferentially to one of the clerks.

Shimada, being the head, had his desk at the far end of the room. The clerks' desks—how many had there been?—were lined up at a right angle to his and extended to the lattice window overlooking the view.

Shimada, then, worked and lived in this long and narrow house. There was no need for him ever to step outside, no need to get wet on a rainy day. All he had to do was to walk the length of the verandah to get to his office and back. It was an extremely convenient arrangement.

As the adopted son of the head Kenzō could afford to be forward with the accommodating clerks. And Shimada, in his dictatorial fashion, would see to it that Kenzō's pranks, which often must have been a great nuisance to the clerks, were tolerated.

Shimada was miserly enough, but his wife Otsune was worse. Some time later, when he had been returned to his original family, Kenzō became accustomed to hearing about her miserliness. ("Talk of lighting a fire with fingernail clippings!") But while living with her, he was unaware of her notorious vice. That she should herself dish out the soup to the maid did not strike him as at all strange. When his own relatives later heard about this habit of hers, they smiled resignedly. "It's a wonder the maid didn't starve to death," they said.

Otsune would put away the leftovers in a cupboard and carefully lock it. On those rare occasions when Kenzō's real father called on them, she would have hot noodles delivered for the guest and the family. After Kenzō's father had left and it was dinner time, she would produce no dinner since they had already had a midafternoon snack. Later Kenzō was shocked to learn that his parents regularly had snacks *and* three meals a day.

But Shimada and Otsune spent a surprising amount of money on Kenzō. He had a very fine haori of yellow silk, for example, which he would wear on their outings together. He could remember having once been dragged all the way to Echigoya, where the Shimadas bought him a length of silk crepe for a new outfit. They had sat in the shop looking at various cloths until closing time. Then what seemed like a horde of apprentices suddenly appeared and started pulling the heavy front doors together. The ominous sight threw Kenzō into a fit of tears.

He had a magic lantern theater, and he would watch in delight the figures dressed in their traditional costumes dancing against the paper backdrop. Once he buried a new top in one of the gutters by the river to give it the proper patina. Fearful of losing it, he would go out several times a day to make sure it was still there, and each time he would stop to poke a stick into a crabs' nest in the embankment. As the little crabs scurried out he would catch some and put them in his pocket.

Thus the Shimadas, so mean in other respects, pampered this child that had been given to them.

41

*B*UT the couple were inwardly uneasy about Kenzō, and constantly demanded reassurances of affection from him. On cold winter evenings as they sat huddled around the brazier they would ask him, "Who is your father?" And Kenzō would point at Shimada. "All right, who is your mother?" Kenzō would look at Otsune and point. The interrogation would not yet be over; only partially satisfied, they would go on to ask, "But who are your real father and mother?" Kenzō, with obvious reluctance, would once more point his finger at one and then the other. Somehow this gave the two pleasure, and they would smile happily at each other.

There were periods when the scene was enacted almost every day, and there were also times when they were not satisfied with this simple interrogation. Otsune was the more persistent of the two. Sometimes she would ask, "Where were you born?" And Kenzō would have to describe the house that he could even now remember—the little house with the red gate and the grove. His answers were of course mechanical, since Otsune had seen to it that they would be precisely what she wanted to hear. But this did not seem to detract from her pleasure at hearing them repeated. "Whose child are you really? Come on, tell me the truth." It was a terrible ordeal for Kenzō. Sometimes he felt more anger than pain, and would stand stiff as a board, refusing to answer. But Otsune would simplemindedly decide that his silence was due to his boyish shyness; she did not know how much he hated her at such times.

The couple did everything in their power to make Kenzō exclusively theirs. They regarded him no doubt as their possession by right. And the more they pampered him, the more possessive they became. He did not mind so much being owned physically, but even his childish heart grew fearful at the thought of becoming emotionally enslaved to them.

They were always careful to make him conscious of their beneficence. He was never allowed to eat a cake or wear a new kimono without being told that it had come from "your father" or "your mother." They seemed not to know that such desperate efforts to win his gratitude would only make him resentful.

Every time he was reminded of what "your father" or "your mother" had done for him, he would immediately want to escape their clutches and be on his own. And he very quickly trained himself to dissociate his favorite toys from the people that had given them to him. The toys had to have an independent existence; otherwise, how could he enjoy them?

They loved him, to be sure, but they did so expectantly, like a rich man who spoils his pretty mistress. Unable to take pleasure merely in being able to reveal their love, they insisted on tangible evidence of its effectiveness. They were being punished for their greed, but this they never realized.

42

IT was not long before Kenzō's character was affected by their behavior. He had originally been a rather meek child. But gradually his meekness came to be replaced by an incorrigible stubbornness, and he was in the end turned into an utterly spoiled brat. Inside a shop or in the middle of a street—it did not matter where—he would squat down and refuse to move if he did not get what he wanted. Once, when being carried on a servant-boy's back, he got hold of the poor fellow's hair and pulled out a handful. And there was the time when he insisted on taking home with him a tame pigeon that he found in the grounds of a shrine.

In the little world created for him by his foster parents he was free to do as he wished, and since this was the only world he knew, he quite naturally assumed that everyone he encountered was there solely to please him. He could not imagine that anyone would refuse to do what he wanted.

Once, however, he had to pay dearly for his impudence. He was awakened one morning as usual by his foster parents. Rubbing his half-closed eyes he walked out to the edge of the verandah. It was his habit to urinate on the garden from there. But that morning he must have been more sleepy than usual, for he fell asleep while urinating. He could not remember falling, but when he woke up again, he found himself lying, unable to move, in the puddle that he himself had made. Unfortunately the verandah was rather far above the ground, since the house, being near the river, was built on a slope. In short, he had dislocated his hip.

Very frightened, the Shimadas took him to a well-known bone specialist for treatment. He had been quite badly hurt, and for many days he lay in bed, his hip covered with some thick yellow ointment that smelled of vinegar. Each morning Otsune would come in and say, "Can't you stand up yet? Try and see." He found that he enjoyed her frustration at his inability to move, and remained in bed far longer than he need have done.

At last he consented to get up, and immediately he walked about the house as though nothing had ever been the matter with his hip. But when he saw the exaggerated way in which Otsune expressed her joy at his recovery, he began to wish that he had stayed in bed a little longer.

Had he been less indulged he might not have been quite so aware of her weaknesses.

Otsune was a practiced hypocrite. She had the convenient knack, for instance, of being able to burst into tears whenever it was in her interest to do so. She had no idea that Kenzō saw through her wiles. She was apt to let her guard down in his company, imagining that subtlety would be wasted on a child.

One day while gossiping with a guest she saw fit to attack a certain woman in the most vicious terms. Kenzō was there, taking it all in. It so happened that after the guest had left this woman dropped in. "Why," Otsune said to her new guest, "I was just telling someone what a wonderful person you were." This was too much for Kenzō. With the outspokenness of a spoiled child he blurted out, "What a lie!"

When the woman had gone Otsune said furiously, "How dare you embarrass me like that in front of a guest!" Kenzō was unmoved. As far as he was concerned, she was getting no more than she deserved. He did not know it, but he was already beginning to loathe her.

It did her no good to love him. There was in her character something so ugly that he could never have returned her love. Unwittingly, by trying so hard to draw him close to her, she had bared more of her ugly self than she had ever done to anyone else.

43

IN the meantime strange things had begun to happen between Shimada and Otsune.

One night Kenzō awoke to find the two reviling each other at his bedside. He was taken aback, and burst into tears.

After this hardly a night passed without their quarreling. Their voices became louder and louder, and finally they went beyond mere exchange of words. He would be awakened by the sound of beating, kicking, and screaming, and would lie there stiff with fright, waiting for it all to end. At first they would stop when they realized he was awake. But after a while they ceased to care what he saw or heard.

He would wonder in utter bewilderment why they fought so regularly and always so late at night. His childish, unknowing mind offered him no answer; all he knew was that he hated what he was forced to witness.

At last Otsune explained the situation to him. This was the story: she herself was a good woman, indeed there was none better; Shimada, on the other hand, was an evil man, but by far the worst was the woman "Ofuji." "That creature," "that thing," she repeatedly called her, her tear-stained face twisted with rage. But her violent misery merely made Kenzō uncomfortable. He felt no sympathy whatsoever.

"She's our enemy, remember that," she said, grinding her teeth, "your mother's and yours. We'll get even with her if that's the last thing we do." Kenzō wanted very much to leave the room.

He was inclined to prefer Shimada, who now spent hardly any time at all in the house and whom he rarely saw during the day, to Otsune, who took care of him from morning till night and who tried so hard to get him on her side.

At some very late hour every night Kenzō would awaken to see in the shadowy light of the night lamp the seated figure of Shimada. His eyes filled with hate, his lips shaking, he would spit out his pent-up venom at his wife.

Even then Shimada would occasionally remember to take Kenzō out. He was not a drinking man, but he was inordinately fond of sweet things. One evening he took Kenzō and Ofuji's daughter Onui to a shop specializing in sweet bean soup. That was the first time Kenzō met Onui. They hardly looked at each other, let alone said anything.

When Kenzō got home Otsune immediately began asking questions. Where had Shimada taken him? Had they stopped at Ofuji's house? Who else had gone to the bean soup restaurant? Notwithstanding Shimada's caution, Kenzō told her everything. But not satisfied, she continued to probe. "That creature was with you, I bet. Come on, tell the truth. If you do, I'll give you something nice. She went with you, didn't she?" Come what may she was going to force a confession out of him. And Kenzō was equally determined not to give in; her contemptible suspicions were no concern of his.

"All right then—what did your father say to the girl? Who did he talk to more—you or her?" With mounting disgust Kenzō looked at her and said nothing. But Otsune was not the sort to know when to stop. "Where did he make you sit in the restaurant—on his right or on his left?"

The jealous woman went on and on. She was incapable of seeing that she was revealing herself shamelessly to her foster child, not yet ten years old, and that by now he was thoroughly fed up with her.

44

SOME time later Shimada went out of Kenzō's life completely. Then the house by the river disappeared too, and Kenzō found himself living alone with Otsune in a strange apartment at the back of a large grocer's. Time had been kind, and he could remember nothing about the place except that it smelled of boiled soybeans.

Otsune talked about Shimada to anybody who would listen, always bitterly and in tears. "I'm going to haunt that good-for-nothing when I'm dead," she would say.

Her violence served only to push Kenzō even further away from herself.

Now that her husband had left her, she became more possessive than ever toward Kenzō. Of course, she had always regarded him as a possession. "Remember," she would say, "I have no one but you now. You mustn't ever let me down—understand?" Awkwardly and ungraciously Kenzō would say something noncommittal. It was simply impossible for him to be the straightforward, obedient boy with her.

Her possessiveness was motivated not so much by affection as by a kind of emotional greed and spite toward another. Young and ignorant though he was, he somehow knew this, and occasionally the knowledge would trouble him. Most of the time, however, he was blissfully indifferent.

Their life together did not last long. What forced their separation, he was never told; perhaps it was poverty or perhaps it was her remarriage. At any rate, one day she disappeared, and he found himself back again with his real parents.

"You know," Kenzō said to his wife, "I can hardly believe I was that boy." For all these years the boy had been a forgotten stranger. And now, under unpleasant circumstances, the boy had forced his way back into Kenzō's consciousness.

"This Otsune," his wife said, "didn't she marry someone named Hatano?" She had no doubt seen the name on the envelope when Otsune wrote that long letter years ago, and even now remembered it.

"I imagine you're right."

"I suppose Mr. Hatano is still living?"

How would he know? He had never laid eyes on the fellow.

"Wasn't he a police inspector?"

"I really don't know."

"But you once told me he was."

"When?"

"That time you showed me her letter."

"Is that so."

A little of the content of the letter came back to him. Otsune had described in boring detail what a difficult baby he had been to care for. Because she had no milk, she had to make special gruel for him every feeding time; he had a weak bladder and was always wetting his bed, et cetera. She had then moved on to the subject of her present situation. A relative of hers, some judge or other living in Kōfu, was kind enough to send her a little money every month; otherwise she really would have been in trouble.

All this he could remember, but not what she had said about her husband. "Maybe he's dead," he said.

"Yes—but it's quite possible he's still alive." Then she added a comment that made him suddenly thoughtful: "We can't be sure, can we, that she won't do exactly what that man did, and pay us a surprise visit?"

45

*T*HE main intention of Otsune's letter had been perfectly obvious to both Kenzō and his wife. The accusation was implicit in everything she said: if a distant relative could be concerned enough to send her money every month, how dare Kenzō, who owed her so much, do nothing at all to help?

Kenzō had sent the letter on to his brother in Tokyo, saying that it was a little embarrassing to have such correspondence addressed to his place of work, and would he ask her not to write again? A reply had come immediately from his brother: she is not your foster mother any more, he said; besides, even if you had remained her foster son, her remarriage alone would have freed you of all responsibility; don't worry, I reminded her of the impropriety of getting in touch with you directly, and she seemed to understand.

Otsune never wrote again. Kenzō was of course relieved, but his conscience was not altogether at ease. He could hardly forget that she had taken care of him once. What made it all so difficult for him was that his dislike for her had by no means lessened. His attitude toward her, in fact, was as confused as his attitude toward Shimada. The only difference perhaps was that in all likelihood he hated her more than he did Shimada.

"To have Shimada bothering us is bad enough," he thought to himself as he gazed at his wife; "what are we going to do if Otsune now comes barging in?" His wife was thinking the same thing, and since they had no claim on her whatsoever, the idea of their intrusion repelled her even more. Besides, her own parents were in trouble, and she had no sympathy to spare for anyone else. Her father had once been a man of position, but now, after too many years in retirement, he was finding it increasingly difficult to make ends meet.

Nowadays, whenever some young man dropped in Kenzō would find himself doing something he had never done before: he would dwell on the contrast between his guest's seemingly carefree life and his own. All these fellows, without exception, seemed so full of hope, so certain of their future. Once he said to one of them, "What fortunate people you are. All you think about is what you will be doing after you graduate."

The young man smiled. "You are assuming, I think, that we are going to be as much in demand as university graduates were in your day. You are wrong, you know. Of course, we are all hopeful that we'll find something we like. But we are perfectly aware that we may not. We've got to be realistic."

The young man was in a sense right. Life was ten times harder now than it had been in Kenzō's student days. But Kenzō was not talking about jobs. "What I meant to say," he said, "is that you fellows are fortunate because you are too young to be weighed down by memories."

The young man looked skeptical. "I am sorry, but you don't look at all like someone who's living in the past. I get the impression that you too are waiting to accomplish something."

Kenzō merely smiled. Then he began talking about some Frenchman's recently published thesis concerning memory. "We've often heard of course that when a man is drowning or falling off a cliff, he is capable of remembering in the few seconds he has left the experiences of his entire lifetime. Well, the Frenchman explains the phenomenon this way: we human beings normally base our lives on anticipation, our minds are filled with thoughts about the future; but if the future is suddenly closed to us, and we realize that we're finished, we look for the first time at our past and gaze at it with a new intentness."

The young man listened with interest. But he could hardly be expected to associate seriously the Frenchman's theory with Kenzō's professed obsession with his own past. Neither was Kenzō so stupid as to imagine seriously that his predicament could be likened to that of a man plunging to his death.

46

SHIMADA, the harbinger of unpleasant memories, appeared again five or six days later.

To Kenzō he was truly a ghost out of the past. But the man sitting before him belonged very much to the present, and no doubt he would cast his shadow on Kenzō's life for some time to come. For how long, Kenzō asked himself uneasily, will this shadow pursue me?

"I took the liberty recently," Shimada said, in a tone as respectful and friendly as before, "of paying Hida a visit." But he refused to make any reference to the reason for his going there. Looking at his bland face one might have imagined that he had called on Hida simply to pass the time of day. "How the neighborhood around there has changed," he continued innocently.

Shimada's behavior quite confused Kenzō. Perhaps the man hadn't really asked Hida to help him get Kenzō back. Or perhaps Hida had not refused the request outright as he claimed. At this point Kenzō did not feel sure about anything.

Shimada seemed unaware of his host's bewilderment. "There used to be a waterfall quite near the house, remember? We went there often in the summer."

Seeing no reason why he should be the one to introduce the unpleasant subject, Kenzō was only too willing to follow the old man's lead in the innocuous conversation.

As he continued, however, Shimada's facade of innocent politeness gradually dropped away, and he began talking of Kenzō's elder sister with gross familiarity. "That woman certainly has aged. I hadn't seen her in years, and I did expect some change, but it was a shock all the same. You wouldn't think now that she had some life in her once. There was a time when she was always picking a quarrel with me. We were always quick to make up, mind you—we were like brother and sister after all. She used to come whining to me for money all the time, I remember. Of course I never turned her away, she was such a sorry-looking creature."

All facts became distorted, Kenzō thought, in this man's malicious and self-centered mind. And how furious Onatsu would be if she could hear what he was saying.

Kenzō sat quietly, staring at Shimada's face. Shimada had an unusually long upper lip. And his mouth had the tendency to hang wide open whenever something aroused his curiosity. He could look a bit of a simpleton, therefore. But no one who saw his deep-set eyes would have taken him for a good-natured one. Even his bushy eyebrows had a mean look about them. His forehead was high and narrow, and as always his hair was brushed straight back without a parting. Kenzō noted with disapproval the sleek and affectedly ascetic hairstyle, and was reminded of religious quacks.

At last Shimada became aware of Kenzō's scrutiny and quickly returned to his earlier formality. He now knew it did him no good to adopt the manner of an older close relative.

In his common, inquisitive way he looked around the room. The walls were shamelessly bare. "Do you like Li Hung-chang's calligraphy?" he asked. "If so, I'll give you one of his scrolls. It's worth a lot of money, I suspect."

Kenzō found it difficult to say yes or no. Once, he remembered, Shimada had got hold of a scroll attributed to Fujita Tōko. It was obviously a fake, of very recent manufacture, and Shimada had hung it over the kitchen hearth to age it. It was extremely unlikely that the Li Hung-chang would be any more genuine.

Seeing that Kenzō was in no mood to be bribed, Shimada finally gave up and left.

47

"WHAT did the man want?" Kenzō's wife seemed to take it for granted that Shimada's visit had not been innocent. Kenzō could hardly blame her.

"I really can't say. It's like a fish talking to a bird."

"What is?"

"I mean Shimada and me, of course. He and I simply don't talk the same language."

Kenzō's wife became quiet. She was thinking of her parents and her husband, who seemed to be moving further and further apart. Kenzō was too stubborn to try to reestablish good relations with his in-laws. He blamed them, and felt that it was up to them to make the first move. On their part, they believed that he had willfully alienated them, and refused to take the initiative. His wife naturally sympathized with her parents. She saw him as a narrow-minded, opinionated professor to whom the rest of the world mattered very little. That she knew she herself was the cause of the animosity between him and her parents made it no easier for her.

She clearly wanted the conversation to end. But Kenzō, whose mind was occupied entirely by thoughts of Shimada, did not sense her mood.

"Don't you think so?" he said.

"Obviously, if you are talking about Shimada and yourself."

"I could hardly be talking about anyone else, could I?"

When he told her about the scroll, she was amused. "Was he really proposing to give it to you?"

"That's what he said."

"I suspect he doesn't really mean it. He may talk about 'giving' it to you now, but I'm sure he intends to use it as an excuse later to squeeze some money out of you. What he's really suggesting is that you buy the thing."

There was no money to buy their growing daughter a decent dress to go out in, she was thinking, let alone some questionable scroll, but of course her husband was indifferent to such things as clothes for the children. Not that it was altogether his fault; after all, he was paying for his recently acquired and much needed raincoat in monthly installments of two and a half yen.

"Then he said nothing about readopting you?"

"That's right. It's all very puzzling. What I can't tell is whether he made the crazy proposal in the first place simply to shock us into seeing him, or whether he was quite serious and when Hida refused decided to give up the idea."

"I wonder which it is?"

"I can't begin to guess. With him, anything is possible."

Three days later Shimada called again. Kenzō was hard at work then, trying to extricate himself from a difficulty which had brought him to a standstill. He had reached the point where with a few more minutes of concentration he might have succeeded. Now his train of thought was interrupted. He turned around and looked at the maid irritably. Not having the courage to refuse to see the most unwelcome visitor, he continued to stare at the poor girl in silence.

"Am I to ask him to come in, sir?"

"I suppose so," he said grudgingly. "And where is my wife?"

"Madame is not feeling too well, and is resting right now."

Was it hysteria again, he wondered, as he tended to do whenever his wife showed signs of fatigue.

He stood up finally and went out to the front to meet his guest.

48

NOT every house in those days had electricity, and their living room now was as usual illuminated by the weak glow of an oil lamp.

The oil cup fitted into a flat, round saucer which rested on a thin bamboo stem. The stem had a round base, about the size of the saucer, so that the entire pedestal looked like a small hand drum.

Shimada had the lamp by him, and was fussing with the wick. Not bothering to look up as Kenzō entered, he said, "The flame needs adjusting. It's smoking too much."

The lamp was a temperamental one, and if the wick was not trimmed with particular care, it would smoke profusely. Noting that its chimney was indeed getting quite black, Kenzō said, "Let's have the maid bring us another one." But the suggestion was received with a marked lack of enthusiasm by Shimada, who now brought his face close to the glass shade with its busy floral design and peered through the transparent patches. "What can be the matter with it," he muttered anxiously.

How like him, Kenzō thought, to be so offended by an inefficient lamp.

Shimada had always wanted everything to be neat and orderly. It was as though he was trying to make up for his own lack of morals by worrying unduly about dust in the corridors and rubbish in the garden. He was in the habit of rushing about with broom in hand, Kenzō remembered, searching for dirt in the remotest corners. And when anything got broken, he would try to mend it himself, no matter how difficult or time-consuming the job. Of course, meanness played a large role here. A copper coin in the hand seemed to Shimada worth much more than time or labor. "We can mend it ourselves," he would say. "To get someone else to do an easy job like that would be a sheer waste of money."

He lived in constant dread of wasting money. That there were other things that could be wasted he seemed never to learn.

"The trouble with him," Ofuji once said to Kenzō, "is that he is too conscientious." This was soon after she and Shimada were married. Naïve as he was then, Kenzō knew that "conscientious" was not the word for Shimada's trouble, and guessing that Ofuji knew it too and was merely trying to defend her husband's reputation, he was decent enough to say nothing at the time.

But now he wondered whether Ofuji was not right in a sense after all. Perhaps the wastefulness of this man's life had indeed been due to a kind of conscientiousness; with capacities far outmatched by his greed, he had spent all these years desperately trying to satisfy it.

With growing pity Kenzō watched Shimada, who was still staring intently at the flame, his sunken eyes almost touching the glass shade. He said to himself, that is what is left of a lifetime. And as he thought of the meaninglessness of this old man's life, he could not help wondering how he himself would grow old.

He had always disliked the word "god." But at this moment he asked himself the question: If god were to look at my own life, would he think it was much different from this greedy old man's?

Shimada had accidentally turned the wick up too high, and the room suddenly became very bright. In a dither he quickly turned it down; now the flame was feebler than ever. "It certainly needs fixing," he said.

Kenzō summoned the maid and asked her to bring another lamp.

49

THAT evening also Shimada treated Kenzō with respectful formality.

He seemed to have completely forgotten about the scroll. And he did not make even the most oblique reference to the subject of Kenzō's readoption.

He tried valiantly to carry on a light conversation. But it was inconceivable that the two should have interests in common to talk about, no matter how lightly. Most of what he said, then, was of so little consequence to Kenzō as to be virtually meaningless.

Kenzō became bored. Yet even in boredom he was wary; his sense of foreboding remained, that one day Shimada would show himself as he really was and openly become mean and demanding.

It was perhaps because of his own tenseness, but he thought that the way Shimada was looking at him now was very different from the way he had peeked into the lamp—the innocent preoccupation had gone, and a new look of cunning, it seemed to Kenzō, had appeared in his eyes. They were the eyes of an old man, dull and sunken, but the dullness could not camouflage the predatory glint in them.

It gave Kenzō no pleasure at all to be so constantly on guard; often he was tempted to make himself utterly vulnerable and let the poor hungry creature have his fill.

In the next room Kenzō's wife moaned, as if in delirium. It was a sound he had become particularly sensitive to. Seeing his anxiety Shimada asked, "Is someone ill?"

"Yes—my wife."

"I'm very sorry to hear that. What is wrong with her?"

Shimada had never seen her. He did not even know who she was, or when she came to Kenzō. He was therefore only being polite, which was perfectly all right with Kenzō. He neither expected nor wanted sincere concern for his wife from this man.

"We've been having nasty weather of late," Shimada said. "She should be very careful."

The children had gone to bed a long time ago, and the maid had apparently retired to the tiny room next to the kitchen. The house was deathly quiet. Kenzō could not bear to think of his wife lying all alone in the silence; he summoned the maid once more and said, "Please go and sit with my wife." With little enthusiasm the girl bowed and left the room.

Kenzō faced his guest again. His inattentiveness was now brutally evident. But Shimada stood his ground, untouched presumably by his host's obvious impatience.

In time even he became exhausted by the monologue, and began reluctantly to coax his buttocks toward the edge of the cushion. "I hope I didn't take up too much of your time," he said. "I hope we can get together again soon." He said no more about Kenzō's wife's illness. Then, as he was about to leave the house, he turned around and said, "I suppose you are usually free in the evenings?" Getting no definite reply from Kenzō he added, "There's a small matter I want to talk to you about." Kenzō remained unresponsive. By the light of the lamp he was holding he could just see the old man's filmy eyes staring at him. The predatory look of the crouching beast was still there. "Well, good night," Shimada said. He opened the door, and walked out into the darkness. There was no light on Kenzō's outer gate.

50

KENZŌ went immediately to his wife's bedside and said, "What's the matter?" She opened her eyes and looked at the ceiling. A lamp had been placed behind a screen, so the room was even darker than the living room. By peering closely Kenzō was just able to see her face. "What's the matter?" he asked again. She still said nothing.

Such a scene had occurred several times during their marriage. But Kenzō was too high-strung to get used to it, and every time it was repeated, he would feel the same degree of uneasiness. He sat down beside her and said to the bored maid, "You can go now." She got up without a word, then from the doorway bowed and said, "Goodnight, sir." Lying on the floor near where she had been sitting was a needle with a red thread trailing from it. Annoyed, he picked it up. Normally he would have called the maid back and scolded her. But this time he gazed abstractedly at the needle in his hand for a while, then stuck it in the screen. He turned to his wife.

She was not looking at the ceiling any more. Her large black eyes seemed not to be focused on anything. They clearly belonged to a living person, yet they seemed without life, as though they had lost touch with the soul. Wide open, they stared at nothing in the near-darkness.

He reached for her shoulder and gently shook her. "Hey," he said. Without replying she turned her head around slowly and looked vaguely in his direction. "Hey, it's me—understand?" As always, the compassion, the sorrow, the suffering that he felt, he could express only in this terse, commonplace fashion. Only he could know that he was begging her to speak to him, to look at him. In his own way, he was indeed praying. He was only too prone to sentimentality, but to be demonstrative about it was quite beyond him.

His wife's eyes suddenly registered awareness. And like one waking from a dream she looked at him and said very slowly, "Oh—it's you." She began to smile, then stopped abruptly when she saw her husband's tense face. "Has the man left?" "Yes." They said no more for a while. She turned around to look at her children, who slept quietly side by side in the bed next to hers, their heads resting on two tiny pillows. "They're sleeping nicely, aren't they?" she said.

Kenzō put his hand on her forehead. "Would you like a cold towel?"

"No, thank you."

"Are you all right?"

"Yes."

"Sure?"

"Yes. You go to bed now."

"I can't. I have too much work to do."

Kenzō returned to his study, where he would work in the lonely silence till the early hours of the morning.

51

*H*E felt wide awake, yet his mind was dull. He had been so close to finding his way out of the fog; now once more he was quite lost in it, groping about helplessly.

He saw his own pathetic figure standing on the podium before all those young men. They would look up and stare intently at the face of this pathetic figure, then solemnly write down all the half-baked comments. He felt he was letting them down badly, and was ashamed; but more painful was his consciousness of the damage being done to his own self-respect. He thought, "Again I'm going to give a bad lecture." He looked at what he had written, and despised it. Often, when his work was progressing nicely, he would in a fit of vanity tell himself, "Well now, I'm not such a fool after all." But at this moment there was not a trace of self-confidence left in him. And his resentment at all the circumstances which prevented his pursuit of a peaceful life of the mind increased.

Finally, he flung his pen down angrily. "I quit—and I don't care a damn." It was past one o'clock. He put out the light and went out into the dark corridor. At the other end was their room with the night lamp still on.

They were all sound asleep—the children huddled together like puppies, his wife lying quite relaxed on her back. As quietly as possible he sat down beside her and peered at her face. Then he put his hand palm down just above her nose, and waited until he could feel the warm breath. At last, when he had made absolutely sure that she was breathing normally, he withdrew his hand. But he was not satisfied. Now he wanted to wake her. He was about to say something to her, but was able to restrain himself. Next he wanted to prod her, but again he resisted the temptation. He managed finally to tell himself, as any other man would have done long before, that she was all right. Even then he was under the illusion that his extreme nervousness was normal under the circumstances.

Sleep was the best medicine for her. Many times Kenzō had sat beside her, waiting patiently for sleep to come to her; and when it did come, he would be filled with gratitude. But when she slept too well he would begin to wonder about those eyes that lay hidden under the closed lids; and he would shake her until she opened them again. She would look at him, exhausted and imploring, and he would be immediately sorry. But he never learned to leave her alone. His state of nerves was such that he required constant reassurance that she was all right.

He changed into his night clothes and crawled into his bed. There he tried to find rest for his dulled yet agitated mind. The night was too far gone perhaps to cure the dullness. But at least it was quiet, and some of the agitation might go by morning.

He heard his wife calling him. As he opened his eyes she said to him, "It's time to get up." She herself was still in her bed, and was holding the pocket watch she had pulled out from under his pillow. In the kitchen the maid was slicing something on the chopping board. "She's awake, I see," he said. "Yes, I just went over to wake her," his wife said. There was no need for her to add that she had then come back to bed. Kenzō got up quickly, and she followed. They said not a word to each other about the night before; it was as though they remembered nothing.

52

SUCH conduct on each other's part they took for granted. They knew—though the knowledge perhaps was not articulated in their minds—that there was a bond between them, albeit a peculiar one, a bond that would have been incomprehensible to an outsider. And it never occurred to them even to wonder whether others might not find their behavior odd.

Kenzō left the house in silence. Several times during work that day he thought of his wife's illness, and of those wide open yet unseeing black eyes, and wanted to stop whatever he was doing and rush back to her. Several times he had the feeling that a messenger would suddenly appear with ill tidings from home.

From one corner of the large lecture hall he would stare vacantly at the door at the other end, or at the high domed ceiling shaped like the inside of a knight's helmet. The square pieces of varnished wood arranged like steps leading up to the top of the dome made it seem even higher than it was, and he would wish forlornly that it would swallow up his agitated soul. His gaze would then wander back to the solemn, black-headed youths seated in rows in front of him, and he would quickly pull himself together.

For all his proneness to such deep anxiety, he was relatively calm where Shimada was concerned. He regarded him as a mean and even potentially dangerous old man, but he was contemptuous of him also, and doubted that he possessed the necessary faculty to put his evil designs into effect. It was only that he resented—perhaps to an abnormal degree—having to waste so much of his valuable time with the man.

"What will he want the next time?" he said to his wife, with more apprehension than he actually felt.

"You know very well what he wants. Instead of worrying so much about it, why don't you simply tell him you're through with him?"

He knew what she said made sense, but didn't say so. "I'm not worried, I tell you. Who in his right mind would be afraid of a creature like that?"

"Of course you aren't afraid of him. But surely it must be an awful nuisance to have to see him?"

"There's a great deal in this world one can't dismiss simply because one thinks it's a nuisance."

He was being a trifle perverse. And perhaps it was in order to maintain an appearance of consistency before his wife that when Shimada appeared again, he agreed to see him despite the fact that he was even busier than usual.

Just as his wife had guessed, the "small matter" that Shimada had wanted to talk about was money. He had tired of waiting for the right opening, which might never have come anyway. With no further attempt at delicacy, he said immediately upon sitting down, "I'm rather short of cash these days. You are the only person I can ask, so please do whatever you can." His tone was demanding, and implied that it was Kenzō's duty to help him. Yet it was not so brazen as to wound Kenzō's pride.

Kenzō went to the study to get his wallet. There never was very much in it, since his wife was in charge of family finances. Often it lay for days on the desk, empty.

Shimada looked a little pained as Kenzō now pulled out the few bills that were in it and put them down in front of him. "I'm sure you need more," Kenzō said as he displayed the inside of his wallet, "but as you can clearly see for yourself, it's all I've got."

When Shimada had gone Kenzō went back to the study without saying anything to his wife. The wallet was left lying on the floor of the living room.

53

*T*HE next day when he came back from work he found the wallet carefully put back on the desk. It was of good leather, large, and perhaps somewhat ostentatious for a man in his situation. He had bought it in a very fashionable street in London. But souvenirs from abroad had long ceased to have much meaning for him, and this particular item had come to seem the most useless of them all. He began to suspect his wife's motives in putting it back in his study with such exaggerated care. He gave the object one sardonic glance, and went to work. For days it was left untouched.

Then came the time when he needed some money. He walked into his wife's room where he found her sewing and pushed the wallet under her nose. "Put a little money in it, will you?" "But it shouldn't be empty," she said, looking up at her husband. She had not questioned him about Shimada's last visit, nor had Kenzō bothered to tell her about it. Assuming therefore that she had not guessed the truth, he said, "There was some money in it, but that's gone. I gave it away." She still seemed not to understand. She laid on the floor the ruler she had been holding, and put out her hand. "Let me see," she said. Impatiently he handed her the wallet. She opened it, then calmly pulled out four or five rather dirty bills and held them up. "See? I was right." She was smiling, and Kenzō thought that in her smile there was a touch of smugness.

"When did you put them in?"

"Oh, after that man left."

It was with curiosity, rather than gratitude, that Kenzō now looked at his wife. The woman he was married to was rarely so understanding. Did she do it, he wondered, out of sympathy for her husband who had been forced to give away money without her knowing? But he did not ask her whether this was so. And his equally obstinate wife was not about to explain. Thus her gift was received in silence and spent in silence.

As time passed her belly got very large. She could hardly move now without being out of breath, and she became increasingly subject to fits of depression. "I'm not sure I'll survive it this time," she would say, crying. Kenzō, who tended to ignore her at such times, would now and again feel obliged to say something. "Why do you say that?" "I don't know—it's just a feeling I have."

Vaguely, in some far corner of their minds, they shared a foreboding. But it was nothing they could put into words. Like the sound of a bell that has faded away into the distance, it was there and it was not there.

She thought of her sister-in-law who had died in childbirth and of her own serious condition after their first child was born. She had not been able to keep her food down, and if the condition had lasted another couple of days, they would have had to feed her anally. How had she managed to live through all that, she now wondered.

"Being a woman isn't much fun," she said.

"Perhaps. But that's how things are." His answer was a lazy one; indeed, when he thought about it, it was no better than a lie.

54

KENZŌ too was subject to sudden changes of mood, and he was not always so ready to pacify his wife, even in that abstracted, mechanical way of his. At times he would be irritated beyond endurance by the sight of her lying cheerlessly on the floor, and from spite would command her to get up and immediately attend to his needs. She would remain where she was, resting her bulging belly ponderously on the floor, and look quite unconcerned. Kick me if you like, she seemed to be saying, see if I care. And in smug silence—she said little at the best of times—she would watch her husband being consumed by rage.

"Impudent, that's what she is," Kenzō would tell himself, conveniently forgetting all her other attributes and rendering her for the time being the personification of impudence. At this personification he would then direct his hatred. But for all the concern she showed, he might as well have hated a fish. Her passivity was seen by observers as a sign of remarkable breeding, whereas his outbursts struck them as irresponsible and a little crazy.

Sometimes he thought he saw a threat in her eyes: "If you go on being mean like this, I'm going to get hysteria again." The threat, imagined or not, filled Kenzō with fear; at the same time, it increased his resentment.

In his heart he hoped fervently that she would stay well, but outwardly he betrayed no concern for her health at all. She saw through the pretense, and occasionally took advantage of his weakness. "Who cares," she would mutter not quite inaudibly, "the baby is going to kill me anyway." And he would feel like shouting, "All right, die, you silly woman!"

One night he woke up to find his wife staring fixedly at the ceiling. In her outstretched hand was the razor he had brought back from Europe. To his relief he saw that at least the blade was still in the ebony sheath. He was frightened nevertheless. "Don't be a fool!" He reached over, grabbed the razor, and flung it across the room. It shattered the glass pane in the sliding door and fell on the verandah outside. His wife remained still all the while, seemingly in a daze.

Kenzō stayed awake, trying to find an explanation for his wife's behavior. Was she so desperately unhappy that she was seriously thinking of killing herself? Or had she suffered an attack and lost control of herself? Or was she resorting to underhanded womanly tricks in her battle with her husband? If so, what did she hope to gain? Greater kindness and understanding from him—or some cheap feeling of victory?

Every once in a while he would glance surreptitiously at his wife's face, hoping to find some clue. But she lay in her bed in perfect imitation of death, and betrayed nothing.

That he should find a satisfactory answer to his questions was to Kenzō of far greater immediate importance than his work. Without it, he had no basis for knowing how he should act toward her. In the old days, when he was much simpler, he readily attributed all instances of abnormal behavior on her part to her illness. And every time she had an attack, he would treat her with near-pious humility, convinced that such would be the way of any loving, considerate husband. Even now his desire to ascertain the cause of his wife's action stemmed from affection and goodwill. But the simple explanation which had once satisfied him did so no longer.

He lay in bed asking himself the same questions over and over again, until at last he dozed off from exhaustion. Not long after he was up, getting ready to go to work. He was in such a hurry that he had no time to speak to his wife about the incident. She made no reference to it either; she moved about the house as though nothing untoward had happened, as though daylight had wiped out all memory of the preceding night.

55

USUALLY after such unpleasant occurrences there would be a period of normalcy to give them the respite they needed, and they would begin talking to each other like other married couples.

But normalcy was like a transient guest in their house, and very quickly they would find themselves once more living with their backs turned toward each other. And when the strain became unbearable Kenzō would order his wife to pack up and go back to her parents. She would look straight back at him, as if to say whether to leave or to stay was her decision to make, not his. Angered by her attitude, he would repeat the order several times.

Once she said, "All right, I'll leave," and did go back to her parents with the children. He was elated by the prospect of being able to live like a young, irresponsible student again. He agreed to send a maintenance allowance every month for her and the children, but apart from that, he could forget about them.

There was now only the maid living with him in the relatively large house. But the sudden quiet gave him no sense of loneliness at all. "How peaceful," he would say to himself, and scribble away from morning to night at a makeshift desk in the large living room. It was in the middle of the summer, and whenever the heat got too much for him—he had little physical endurance—he would throw himself down on the shabby, yellowed mat and rest, finding strangely pleasant the smell of old straw that seemed to steam out of it and penetrate his body.

His handwriting was spidery, shriveled, as though it too had been affected by the heat. His notes were more copious than need be, for the work gave him pleasure. But it was a strain also, and he was doing it because his job demanded it.

The maid's father was a gardener. One day she brought back a couple of potted plants for her master and put them on the verandah outside the morning room where it was her custom to chat with him as she served his breakfast. Her thoughtfulness delighted him, but not the plants. They were the kind one could buy for thirty sen in any market, with the pot thrown in.

He worked on, happily forgetful of his wife's existence. He had no desire to visit her, nor did he worry about her illness. "She's with her parents," he told himself. "If anything serious happens they'll let me know." He was enjoying the kind of peace that would have been unattainable had she been with him.

He made no effort to see either her relatives in town or his own. And they on their side left him alone. He worked all day, took walks in the cool of the evening, then crawled under the green, patched-up mosquito net and went to sleep.

A month passed, and his wife appeared without warning. He had just gone out to their modest garden to take a stroll under the early evening sky. He was near the verandah outside the study when suddenly the half-collapsed wicket was pushed open and she came in. "Have me back, won't you?" she said simply.

Her clogs, Kenzō noticed, were very down-at-heel and even beginning to split at the edges. Feeling sorry for her, he brought out his wallet and took out three yen. "Here, go and buy some new clogs. You can't go around looking like that."

A few days later his mother-in-law came to see him. She had little to say, except to repeat her daughter's simple request somewhat more formally. Kenzō agreed without hesitation, thinking that it would be senselessly cruel to refuse. After all, if she really wanted to come back, why shouldn't she?

But alas, her manner after her return was exactly as it had been before, and Kenzō began to nurse the feeling that somehow he had been cheated by his mother-in-law. The more he thought about it, the more resentful he became, and finally he found himself asking, "How much longer is this going to last?"

56

SHIMADA continued to call on Kenzō, to make sure his existence would not be forgotten. Who knows, he no doubt thought, generosity might become a habit with Kenzō. And indeed there were several occasions when Kenzō was obliged to go the the study to fetch his wallet.

"That's a fine wallet," Shimada once said. "You can tell it's not Japanese—there's something about it that's different." He picked it up and examined it admiringly. "Forgive me for asking, but how much was it?"

"Ten shillings, I think. That would be about five yen."

"Five yen? That's quite a price. There's a fellow in Asakusa whom I've known a long time—he would make one for you for a lot less. Next time you need one, let me know, and I'll speak to him."

The wallet was never full. Sometimes it would be quite empty, and at such times Kenzō had no choice but to stay put in the living room, waiting impatiently for the old man to go, and getting angrier and angrier. "Will the creature never leave? Can't he tell I've got no money to give him?" But no matter how exhausting the waiting game might become, he refused to go to his wife for the money. And she, on her part, never said a word to him about the "gifts," presumably thinking that the sums involved were not yet worth fussing about.

In time, however, Shimada became more openly demanding, and began asking for quite substantial sums, such as twenty or thirty yen. With no apparent consciousness of his own crudeness, he said on one occasion, "How about it now. You're talking to a childless old man, remember, who has only you to depend on." Kenzō, offended, said nothing. With his dirty, sunken eyes Shimada looked slyly at him, then muttered, "No one's going to tell me a man who lives like this can't afford a mere twenty yen."

When Shimada had gone Kenzō said to his wife with distaste, "The initial frontal assault having failed, he's now trying to starve me out slowly. He couldn't get a large lump sum, so he's going to squeeze it out of me in installments. He is absolutely despicable."

When in a rancorous mood, Kenzō was apt to use such words as "absolutely" and "extremely." His wife, perhaps because of her slow, obstinate nature, was in this respect more controlled. She said, "It was your fault in the first place. You should have been firm right from the start—you should never have let him get near you."

Kenzō's face went stiff. Her comments were unnecessary and obvious. "If I had wanted to keep him away from the house, I would have done so."

"But what have you gained from seeing him?"

"Your point of view is bound to be different, since you have no connection with him. I am not you."

She somehow managed to misunderstand him. She said, "Of course. As far as you're concerned, I'm nothing but a stupid woman." Kenzō decided that it was too much trouble to explain what he had meant.

During those periods when there was little sympathy between them, even the simplest remarks could not be exchanged without misunderstanding. Still carrying in his mind the sinister figure of Shimada as he left the house, Kenzō went to his study and there he sat down to brood. His wife went about her business, tired of this husband of hers who continued to remain aloof from his family. If he wanted to shut himself off in his miserable cell, she was not the one to stop him.

57

KENZŌ felt as though his head was stuffed with crumpled paper. His irritability was such that sometimes he thought he would go mad unless he gave vent to it. Once for no reason at all he kicked a pot of flowers that belonged to the children off the verandah. It was a prize possession of theirs, something their mother had bought them after days of begging on their part. The sight and sound of the red pot smashing as it hit the ground gave Kenzō some satisfaction. But when he saw the broken stem and the torn flowers he was momentarily overcome with sadness at the useless, cruel thing he had done. These pitiful flowers, he thought, had seemed beautiful to the children, and now their own father had destroyed them.

He felt some remorse, but he could not bring himself to go to the children and confess. And there was the usual rationalization that he could fall back on: "It's not my fault—it's hers. If I act like a madman sometimes, it's because of her."

A calm, leisurely conversation with someone friendly would have helped to soothe his nerves. But to Kenzō, who had customarily gone out of his way to avoid people, a suitable companion was not readily available. And so he smouldered alone.

When the maid would appear with the visiting card of someone like an insurance agent—who would not have been welcome at the best of times—he would angrily scold the innocent girl in a voice loud enough to be heard by the caller. Later he would be ashamed, angry at himself for his inability to treat ordinary harmless people like an insurance agent with a modicum of graciousness and goodwill. At the same time he would again console himself, almost proudly, with his fond excuse: "It's not my fault, and even if that fellow doesn't know, at least *I* know."

Because he had no faith, he could not say, "At least god knows." In fact, the thought that he might be happier if he could never occurred to him. Morality for him was something that began and ended with himself.

Sometimes he thought about money. There were even times when he wondered why he had not chosen wealth as the goal in his life. He was vain enough to believe that had he really wanted to, he could have made as much money as the next man.

He looked at the mean way in which he and his family lived, and felt there was not much sense in it. He thought about his relatives who were even poorer than he, who were struggling even harder to stay alive, and was sorry for them. He pitied Shimada too, who toiled from morning to night to satisfy what was after all a rather modest ambition. Everybody wants money, he thought, and nothing else. And he began to wonder whether they were not perhaps right.

He had never been good at making money, partly because it had always seemed to him to require an inordinate amount of time. After graduation, he had turned down all sorts of offers and gladly accepted a teaching job that paid only forty yen a month. Half of the salary he had had to hand over to his father. With the rest, he had lived contentedly in a shabby room in a temple, eating nothing but potatoes and fried bean curd. But despite the discomforts he had willingly accepted for the sake of freedom, he had accomplished little.

Kenzō as he was now and the young graduate of those days were different in many ways. But in that he was still poor and still waiting to do something worthwhile, they remained alike.

He was beginning to tire of being neither rich nor accomplished. But it was too late for a man as ignorant of the ways of the world as he to start trying to make money. On the other hand, he was beset by too many worries to do well what he wanted to do. And whenever he asked himself what was the main cause of these worries, the answer always seemed to be money.

He felt quite lost, not knowing where to turn. The day when he would possess something substantial in its own right, something that made money irrelevant, seemed at this point to be very far away.

58

*I*MMEDIATELY on returning to Japan Kenzō had begun to be short of money. By the time he had settled in a new house in his native Tokyo after years of absence, he didn't have a penny to his name.

During his stay abroad, his wife and children lived in a cottage that stood in her father's grounds. Though small it was dignified enough. Her grandparents had occupied it until their death, and had given it a touch of old-world elegance; the sliding doors, for instance, still had pasted on them sketches and calligraphy by late Edo masters.

Her father was a civil servant. He was not able to lead a stylish life exactly, but his means were sufficient to enable him to support his daughters without difficulty. Besides, the government sent her an allowance every month, and Kenzō was able to leave her behind with a clear conscience.

While Kenzō was abroad there was a change in the cabinet, and his father-in-law was obliged to leave a relatively safe sinecure for a more prominent but exposed post. Unhappily the new cabinet was very short-lived, and the poor man's career fell with it.

When the news reached Kenzō he was sorry, but thought it hardly necessary to worry about his father-in-law's future livelihood; and even when he returned he continued briefly to hold his naïvely optimistic view of the old man's financial situation. Moreover, he really believed that the family allowance of twenty yen from the government had been sufficient for his wife, the two children, and the maid. "With no rent to pay, it must have been more than enough."

Very soon, however, the truth dawned on him, and he was shocked. During his absence, his wife had worn out all of her day clothes and had been forced to restyle some of his, dull-colored and mannish though they were, for her own use. The bed mats had hardly any stuffing left in them. The counterpanes were tattered. And her father had had to let her live in this state, unable to help. He had taken risks on the stock market after losing his position, and his modest savings had dwindled almost to nothing.

Kenzō, always vain about his appearance, had returned wearing a collar so fashionably stiff and high that he could barely move his head to get a good look at his wife and children in their rags. The contrast between himself and them might have struck him as funny had it not been quite so bitterly ironical.

His crates arrived a few days later. They were filled with books and contained not one trinket for his wife. He began to feel really foolish when he realized that the cottage was so small it could not house even one crateful of his books. Immediately he began looking for a house.

But moving into a new house cost money. The first thing he did was to resign his position, which he had retained throughout his stay abroad; this got him severance pay, at the rate of half a month's salary for every year of service. It did not amount to much, naturally, but it enabled him to buy the necessary furnishings for the new house.

With the modest sum of money in his pocket he had walked from shop to shop with an old friend who was a fanatical price-haggler. They must have looked at hundreds of tea trays, ash trays, braziers, and bowls that day, and walked a countless number of miles. In a commanding voice the friend would order the shopkeeper to accept a certain price, and if the order was not obeyed—as was more often the case than not—he would stalk out of the shop, leaving Kenzō behind. Having no choice in the matter, Kenzō would run after him. If Kenzō happened to show some inclination to linger in the shop, he would shout at him from a block away, "Hey, what do you think you're doing!"

The friend was a kind man, but when it came to shopping—whether for himself or for another—he lost his balance and became quite violent.

59

KENZŌ had had some bookshelves and a desk made too, by a mean-minded carpenter who specialized in Western-style cabinetwork. He could remember how he had stood outside the shop, discussing prices with that walking abacus, so clearly bent on making every sen he could out of the deal.

The bookshelves were unpaneled at the back and had no glass doors. But he was hardly in a position to start worrying about dust on his books. The wood was unseasoned, and the shelves sagged under the weight of heavy English tomes.

But the process of acquiring even such pitiful pieces of furniture took time. And very quickly the money, for which he had given up his job, was gone. In wonderment he looked around his new house: how could it be still so desolate?

Then, as perverse fate would have it, a most unwelcome letter arrived. It was from an old acquaintance who had been abroad at the same time as Kenzō and who had lent him money when he badly needed some new clothes. If convenient, it said, would Kenzō pay back the debt now? For a long while he had remained seated at his new desk, staring helplessly at the letter.

Kenzō had vivid enough memories of the man, though they had not been together long in the foreign country. They had been to the same university in Tokyo, not so many years apart. But that was about all they had had in common. The man had been sent abroad as an official observer, a proud representative of his government, and the difference between his stipend and Kenzō's was so great as to be laughable.

They stayed in the same lodging house for a time. The man's apartment had a living room in addition to the bedroom, and in the evenings he would appear in an embroidered satin dressing gown, sit down contentedly in front of the fire, and read. Kenzō, who lived like a frightened mouse in a cell-like room that faced the north, secretly envied him.

Kenzō remembered too with some sadness how he had sometimes economized on his lunch. Once he bought a sandwich on his way back to the lodging house and munched it as he wandered about aimlessly in a large park. In one hand he held his umbrella, with which he tried to ward off the rain that blew toward him at a slant; in his other hand he held the slices of bread with the thinly cut meat between them. It was very difficult to eat like that, and more than once he hesitated before a bench, wondering whether he should sit down. But the benches were all soaking wet.

Sometimes he would open a tin of biscuits in his room and chew the dry, crumbly things until they felt wet enough to go down his throat. If he had had some hot water even, it would not have been such an ordeal.

At other times he would eat meager one-course meals in questionable restaurants patronized by cabmen and laborers. They sat at a long counter, with the wall rising sheer immediately behind their backs. One could not gape about therefore, as in an ordinary restaurant. But if one wanted to, one could see at a glance all the other customers seated in a row on either side. Their faces looked as though they had not been washed for days.

The acquaintance must have taken pity on his unfortunate compatriot, for he would often take him out to lunch or to the local public bath, and at tea time invite him up to his apartment.

They had thus become quite familiar when Kenzō asked for a loan of ten pounds. With impressive nonchalance the man handed him two five-pound notes. Of course he did not deign to ask when he might have it back. Kenzō, in response to the apparent casualness of the other, decided he need not worry about the debt until they were back in Japan.

After his return, then, Kenzō had continued to regard it as an obligation that could be temporarily put aside until the other party reminded him of it. And so when the reminder did come, Kenzō was caught unprepared.

Not being able to think of a better recourse, he went to an old friend. He knew that this man was not particularly rich, but at least he was not in desperate straits. Happily the man somehow managed to scrape up the necessary amount. Agreeing to pay back his new creditor in monthly installments of ten yen, Kenzō rushed off to settle the debt incurred in a distant land.

60

*I*T was in this shabby way that Kenzō had at last settled down in Tokyo.

He did not mind being poor so long as he believed himself to be superior in other respects. But his self-confidence could not but be affected by the constant worrying about money, and in time he began to have serious doubts about his condition. Even his formal kimono of cotton, which he had previously worn without a second thought, came to seem a reminder of his own failure. "It's incredible," he thought to himself, "that anyone should come to *me* for money." And of the cadgers he was thinking of, Shimada clearly was the worst.

It was an undeniable fact that no matter how one looked at it, Kenzō was a more successful man than Shimada. But it was equally undeniable that this fact gave Kenzō no sense of accomplishment whatsoever; that Shimada, who had once called him "Kenbō," should now address him so respectfully afforded him not the slightest satisfaction. Rather, it made him angry to think that Shimada should regard him, of all people, as a source of additional income.

Once he asked his sister, "Tell me, how hard up is he really?"

"Well now, since he comes to you so often, it's possible that he is as poor as he says. But of course, even you with your income can't go on giving him money indefinitely."

"Do I seem well-off?"

"Well, compared to us you are, aren't you?"

In her usual talkative way she began telling Kenzō about her own situation in detail: Hida never brought home his salary intact; the salary was low, but his social expenses were high; because he spent so many hours at the office, he had to eat out often, which cost money; if it hadn't been for the recent half-year bonus, they would have been in real trouble. "And don't you think he came home with all of the bonus. True, we're retired folk more or less, and what we do now is hand over to Hiko-san money for food, and he takes care of the rest, so we shouldn't do too badly."

They were living like independent boarders with their adopted son. Apparently they had their own sugar, rice cake, and so on, which were kept separate from their son's; if they entertained any of their friends in the house, the expense was paid for out of their own household account.

Such an extreme example of economic individualism, Kenzō thought he had never encountered before. But as far as his sister was concerned, theirs was a perfectly natural style of living.

"You're lucky you don't have to scrape along the way we do," she said. "With your ability, you have only to do a bit of work to get all the money you want." She seemed to have forgotten that Shimada had been the original subject of conversation. With a reminder from Kenzō, however, she finally returned to it. "It's not all that serious. If he becomes too much of a nuisance just tell him you'll give him something when it's more convenient. If that doesn't satisfy him, then say you're not at home. You can't afford to be meticulous with a man like that."

The advice was typical of his sister. Having learned nothing from her, Kenzō next got hold of Hida and asked again, "How hard up is Shimada really?"

"He has enough," said Hida. "Don't forget, he's kept the land and the house. Besides, Ofuji gets money regularly from her daughter Onui. I wouldn't believe a word he says, if I were you. Just ignore him."

Hida too was talking off the top of his head.

61

*I*N the end he went to his wife. She was lying on the floor, in a generally untidy condition, as though she had been dragged down by the weight of the child that was due soon. "What sort of situation is Shimada really in? Neither my sister nor Hida seems to know."

She moved her head slowly on the red-lacquered wooden pillow, which was almost hidden by her disheveled hair, and looked up at him without interest. "If it worries you so much, why don't you try more direct ways of finding out? How can she be expected to know a thing like that anyway? She isn't exactly a bosom friend of Shimada's, is she."

"I don't have the time to go around finding out things like that myself."

"In that case, forget about it."

Act like a man was what she really meant. She herself had always refrained from nagging at her husband even about matters that touched her very deeply, such as the animosity between him and her parents. That she should show little open interest in his dealings with Shimada, which she considered hardly her business, was therefore to be expected. Nor was it any less characteristic of her to find his inability to keep his little anxieties to himself both perverse and cowardly.

"What do you mean, forget about it? Did I ever bring the question up before now?" With these angry words Kenzō stalked out of the room.

On occasion the dialogue would take a different turn and last longer.

"I hear Onui has a disease of the spine," Kenzō said to his wife one day.

"That must be hard."

"It's fatal, apparently. Shimada is worried, of course. If she dies, Shibano will have no further obligation toward Ofuji, and the money may very well stop coming."

"How sad for Onui. She must still be quite young."

"She's a year older than I am—didn't I tell you?"

"Does she have any children?"

"Quite a number, I believe. Exactly how many, I don't know."

Kenzō's wife tried to imagine what it must be like for this poor woman, not yet forty, to have to leave behind all those ungrown children. Then she thought of her own pregnancy, and wondered how she herself would fare. With sadness and envy she now looked at the male sitting opposite, who seemed quite untouched by the sight of her swollen belly.

Kenzō had no suspicion of what was going through his wife's head. "No wonder Shimada is worried," he continued. "He never did get on with the Shibanos, you know. It's all Shibano's fault, Shimada will tell you, naturally; according to him, the man's a hot-tempered drunk who'll never get promoted. But I suspect if there was any disapproving, it was the other way around—the Shibanos probably got fed up with Shimada a long time ago."

"But with all the goodwill in the world Shibano couldn't do much for Shimada surely? He has his own children to think of."

"Quite so. Being a soldier, he can't be any better off than I am."

"By the way, how did that man and Ofuji...." She hesitated; then seeing that her husband had in no way understood, she became more explicit: "How did Shimada manage to get to know Ofuji so well?"

As a child Kenzō had heard the story: one day a young widow appeared at the ward office on some business or other; she was obviously not accustomed to dealing with officials, and Shimada, taking pity on her, was kind to her; this was the beginning of their relationship, which ended with Shimada divorcing Otsune and marrying her.

The old story, when he thought about it, left Kenzō a little skeptical; somehow, no matter how broadminded he tried to be, he could not quite imagine Shimada falling in love.

"Greed must have played a part," he said to his wife. She said nothing.

62

*T*HE news that Onui was suffering from an incurable illness brought a touch of gentleness to Kenzō's heart. They had not seen each other for years; moreover, even during the period when their paths used to cross, they had very rarely talked. Strictly speaking, then, theirs had been a superficial acquaintanceship. Yet, perhaps because she had left no deep impression on his mind, he treasured her memory far more than he did Shimada's or Otsune's. That vague abstraction known as humanity seemed temporarily to gain reality through Onui, and he discovered that there still remained in his hardened heart a capacity to feel affection for his own kind.

And so it was with true sympathy that Kenzō thought of Onui lying on her deathbed. Yet his concern for her was not entirely unselfish, for he was certain that her death would provide Shimada with an additional reason for soliciting money. He wished in anticipation that somehow an encounter with Shimada thus fortified could be avoided, but he was constitutionally incapable of devising some plan whereby his wish would be fulfilled.

There was no choice, he decided resignedly, but to continue to see Shimada until a violent head-on clash put an end to the whole unpleasant business. Almost pugnacious now, he waited expectantly for the next visit.

He was therefore somewhat deflated—and of course surprised— when the person who soon appeared on his doorstep turned out to be not Shimada but the old man's sworn enemy, Otsune.

His wife came into the study to announce the visitor: "That Hatano woman has finally come." Looking more pained than surprised, he said nothing. Impatient at his seeming indecisiveness, she said, "Are you going to see her?" If you aren't, she was really saying, say so and be done with it. "Show her in," Kenzō said curtly, and watched her as she pulled herself up with great difficulty.

Kenzō entered the living room to find a poorly dressed woman sitting stiffly, like a prospective employee. Her manner, as she greeted him, was much more respectful than Shimada's. From the way she bowed and spoke to him, one might have thought he was some kind of lord.

He remembered the stories she used to tell when he was a child about her house in the country. The house and the grounds, according to her, were of extraordinary beauty. Artificial streams ran in all directions under the raised floor of the house. (This particular feature she never tired of describing.) And the pillars were supposed to be of nandin wood. But one thing he never learned, and that was where exactly this great mansion was. She herself never went back there all the time Kenzō knew her, let alone took him to see it. As he got older and learned to be more cynical about her, he began to suspect that the house was yet another of her big lies.

That loud woman, he thought, with all those desperate pretensions, had turned into this shamefaced, gray haired woman, and he had to wonder at the changes that time wrought in people.

She was still as fat as ever; nevertheless, she had changed beyond all recognition. There was now not a trace of city-living left in her; to put it crudely, she looked like one of those peasant vendors who wander into the city from some nearby village, carrying baskets on their backs.

63

OTSUNE too was struck by the change in Kenzō as he came into the room. But she at least had had time to prepare herself for the meeting, whereas he had been given only a moment's notice.

Kenzō managed to hide his surprise all the same. Habit alone would probably have given him the needed control. But in addition there was the fear that a show of emotion from him would encourage her to indulge in vulgar theatrics—and having to witness that all over again would have been unbearable. For her sake and his own, he wanted at all costs to avoid any painful display of her weaknesses.

She recounted to him the main events of her life since they had last seen each other. She had had her misfortunes, but no more it seemed, than the ordinary share of them. When it became clear that they would have no children of their own, she said, she and Hatano adopted a girl. Later this girl married a man who had a wine shop, and who was also adopted into the family. (Whether this had happened immediately before or years after

Hatano's death, Otsune did not say; nor did she indicate what kind of a living they had managed to eke out of the shop—it could not have been much of an establishment—except to say bravely that it had been located in a very busy quarter of Tokyo.) Soon after, the man was killed in the war. Not being able to run the shop themselves, the two women had to close it and go to live with a distant relative in a small village not far from Tokyo. Thanks to the modest government pension they were getting, they were more or less able to manage.

Otsune told her story with surprising restraint—hardly any exaggerated gestures, melodramatic expressions, or sly hints. Yet despite this, Kenzō remained quite unmoved. When she had finished he could only say, "Well now, that's too bad." Not even a stranger would have found the half-hearted comment sufficiently polite, but Kenzō, as he uttered it, did not at all feel the inappropriateness of it. At the same time, the very fact that he could not feel more for the woman saddened him, and he said to himself, "The past has put a curse on us."

He was not a man who wept easily. But he was inclined sometimes to wish that an occasion would arise, or a person come before him, that could force tears out of him. He now looked at the pathetic old woman who many years ago had ceased to move him, and wanted to say, "I am not as hard as I seem. For the right person, I too could shed a few tears."

He pulled out five yen from his wallet and put it in front of her. "Forgive me, but I thought you might want to go home by rickshaw." At first she declined, saying that she had not come for anything like that, but in the end she took it. There had been no affection in Kenzō's gesture—only a kind of impersonal pity. This she seemed to know, and she looked at him resignedly as if to say, "Our hearts parted a long time ago, and I was wrong to think they could be brought together again."

As he stood at the front door and watched her walk away he thought, "That shabby woman was once my foster mother. Had she been more decent, I would at least have tried to console her. And I would have been with her when she died."

How he felt then, no one could know.

64

"SO grandma has made her appearance at last," said Kenzō's wife with unaccustomed jocularity. "Grandpa has a partner now—he doesn't have to haunt you all by himself anymore."

Kenzō was not sure whether she was merely being cheerful or being funny at his expense. At any rate he was in no mood to respond.

Not discouraged she added, "I suppose she talked about that again."

"I am afraid I don't understand."

"About your having a weak bladder, of course, and what a lot of trouble you were to grandma."

There was not a trace of a smile on Kenzō's face. But he did in truth wonder why that garrulous Otsune had not mentioned it.

Otsune had always had a highly developed sense of self-preservation, her principal weapon being her verbal virtuosity. He remembered that his father, a credulous and easily flattered man, was constantly being taken in by her. "What a fine woman Otsune is," he would say. "A model wife, that's what she is." And when she fell out with Shimada, she put on a performance for him that was most successful. Profoundly moved by her weeping and teeth-gnashing, he had immediately become the staunchest of her allies.

Kenzō's sister also had been an accomplished flatterer, and therefore their father's favorite. Whenever she came to him for money, the old man would grumble, but purely for form's sake. He would fetch his money box in the end and give her whatever she asked for. And after she had departed, he would say to the others in the house defensively, "With a husband like Hida, what can she do?"

But even she had been no match for Otsune. She simply could not approach the other in plausibility. At the age of sixteen or so, Kenzō had suddenly realized that of all the people who knew Otsune, he alone saw through her verbal smoke screen. Her skill was indeed phenomenal.

No wonder, then, that his first reaction on hearing that Otsune had come to the house had been to wince at the thought of having to listen to her talk. "If I may say so, I was the one that had to bring you up," he could imagine her saying, and then enlarging on the tiresome subject for hours. Or "Shimada is your enemy," she might say, and this particular obsession, like the theme of some banal moving picture, would be restated ad nauseam.

She was bound to cry too. There would be the right amount of tears, precisely measured, released at the right dramatic moment. She was not like his sister, true, in that she rarely raised her voice. But when required her voice would become unpleasantly theatrical, with a calculated rise there and a drop here in her intonation. She reminded one, in fact, of heroines in those nineteenth-century melodramas who were invariably pictured sitting by a brazier, tearfully recounting the wrongs done to them and now and then sticking the poker into the ashes to emphasize a point.

Her conduct during the interview, then, had been totally out of character; so much so that it had left him more bemused than grateful. His wife tried to ease his mind: "Don't forget, almost thirty years have passed since she knew you well, and even she is bound to behave with some reticence after so many years. And people forget things after a time; what bothered her before needn't bother her now. Besides, a person's character can change, you know."

But Kenzō's conception of Otsune had become too crystallized to be modified by the experience of one isolated encounter. And so he listened to his wife skeptically, telling himself that Otsune was too devious a character to be explained away quite so simply.

65   *K*ENZŌ'S wife laughed at his unwillingness to concede that Otsune might have changed. That she herself did not know Otsune seemed to make no difference to her. "You really are incorrigible," she said with conviction. He has always been like this, was her thought; he is just as opinionated where my parents are concerned.

"It's not me that's incorrigible," he said. "It's that woman. You wouldn't talk such nonsense if you knew her."

"But you yourself admitted she was not at all like what she used to be. Surely that's enough reason to change your mind about her?"

"I'm trying to tell you that the difference is only on the surface. I would gladly change my mind if I thought she really had reformed."

"But how can you tell after one short meeting?"

"I can tell even if you can't."

"You're being rather arbitrary, if you ask me."

"All right, then, I'm being arbitrary. But what does it matter, so long as I'm right?"

"But what if you're wrong? You can hurt a lot of people that way. Not that it bothers me, really. After all, I don't know the woman."

Kenzō knew that in ostensibly talking about Otsune, she was in fact defending her parents. But this was as far as she would go; she was not clever enough, she felt, to carry on a verbal battle with her husband to the very end. "Oh, what's the use," she would say to herself, and rather than talk, she would bear with all the unpleasantnesses that resulted from unfinished discussions. But such forbearance gave neither of them very much satisfaction.

They hated each other's obstinacy; yet, sensing the seething resentment that the other secretly harbored, each was forced to acknowledge there was good reason for it.

In his willful fashion Kenzō had for some time refused to visit his in-laws. And she, with her obstinate defeatism, had simply shrugged her shoulders: "Oh, what's the use—I've done all I can."

That was always his inner retort too: "I've done all I can." But happily, when the tension reached a certain point, the two from necessity would unwind themselves and treat each other with more gentleness. Once, when her pregnancy was not so advanced, she had taken hold of his hand and put it on her belly. "Can you feel it move? Whose child is it, I wonder." On another occasion she had said, "You know, we shouldn't quarrel so much. We're both being very irresponsible." Not at all sure that he had been in any way irresponsible, Kenzō had smiled awkwardly; then with great solemnity he had said, as though no one before him had ever had the same thought, "When people who have been close don't see each other for a time, they become strangers. But when two people live together, no matter how bad things may get between them, they somehow manage to stay close. I suppose human beings are made that way."

66

*B*ESIDES Shimada and Otsune, there were his brother and sister to think of.

Chōtarō's health always broke down when the weather got cold. This year too, at the beginning of autumn, he caught a bad chill. He stayed at home for a week, then despite the fact that he had not fully recovered, went to the office. He was now in bed as a result, suffering from a persistent fever. "I shouldn't have gone to work, I know," he said, "but I felt I had to." He knew he should take better care of himself if he wanted to live, but taking care of himself necessarily meant to be without work and money. "They tell me it looks like pleurisy," he said forlornly. He was more afraid than anyone of dying, and it was his misfortune that he could not resign himself to his fate, which was to be possessed of a rapidly decaying body.

Kenzō said to his wife, "He says he has to go back to work soon. Surely he can wait until the fever goes away."

"Obviously he would like to, but I suppose he can't afford not to work."

Sometimes, when thinking about Chōtarō's family, Kenzō was apt to worry only about their livelihood if Chōtarō should die. It was a cruel way to think, and though he forgave himself for it, thinking it natural and necessary, he could not help feeling angry at his own mercenariness.

"You don't think he'll die, do you?"

"Hardly," his wife said, refusing to take Kenzō's question seriously. She was too preoccupied with her own condition to worry about other people's discomforts.

Her midwife was some kind of relative. She would from time to time pay a call, having traveled a great distance by rickshaw. Wondering what she did when she came, Kenzō once asked his wife, "Tell me, does she massage you?" "Something like that," she answered, not without contempt.

Then Chōtarō's fever suddenly went away. "He tried incantation, apparently," reported Kenzō's wife. She had great faith in the supernatural, and all forms of devotional practice impressed her.

"I suppose you encouraged him."

"Oh no. What he had to do was something I never heard of—you put a razor on your head, you see, and keep it there during the incantation."

Kenzō hardly knew what to think. Finally he said, "He probably convinced himself that he was ill in the first place, and now he's convinced himself he's better. A ladle or pot lid on the head would have done just as well."

"Anyway, it seems he got tired of having to pay for all that medicine, and when someone suggested calling this priest in, he thought he might as well give it a try. I don't suppose the ceremony cost very much."

Kenzō thought his brother a fool. But when he remembered that in all probability the medicine had proved much too expensive, he was sorry. Razor or no razor, the important thing was that his brother was better.

Soon after his brother's recovery, his sister was seized with asthma. "Oh no, not again," Kenzō blurted out. Then he immediately thought of Hida, who would not allow his wife's misery to upset him in the least.

"Your brother says it's worse than it's ever been. He thinks you ought to go and see her, just in case anything happens." When she had given the message Kenzō's wife awkwardly lowered herself to the floor. "When I stay on my feet any length of time my belly begins to feel funny. And I wouldn't dream of reaching for something on a shelf nowadays."

Kenzō was surprised. He had always imagined that the further advanced the pregnancy, the more active a woman had to be. Discouraged by his own ignorance, he gave up all thought of urging her to move about more.

"I couldn't possibly visit her," she said.

"Of course not. I'll go myself."

67

KENZŌ now was always exhausted when he came home. And because of his exhaustion—which was not entirely due to overwork, he was sure—he became more sedentary than ever. He took naps constantly. Sometimes he would even fall asleep while reading at his desk; he would then awaken with a start and get back to work with renewed desperation. Very soon he became so conscious of the time he was wasting that all his waking hours at home he spent in his study. To sit glued to his desk in this way lessened his sense of guilt, no matter how little was being accomplished.

Four or five such wasteful days went by and at last he managed to drag himself off to visit his sister. He felt like a fool when he discovered, on arriving at her house in Yotsuya, that she was already recovering. Nevertheless, he was able to say with some show of sincerity, "That's good news—congratulations."

"Thank you," she said. "Not that it matters very much what happens to a useless old woman like me. What good am I to anybody anyway? I'm just a burden to everybody, that's all. But I suppose I haven't completed my allotted span, as they say."

She seemed to be inviting pleasantries, if not fervent denials, from Kenzō. But he said nothing, and kept on puffing his cigarette. There was a decided lack of communication between these two, even about the pettiest matters. "But so long as Hida is alive," she continued, "I've got to keep going, however sickly and worthless I may be. He needs me, you see."

Her wifely devotion was a favorite topic of conversation among relatives. In view of Hida's unforgivable callousness toward her, it was perhaps more pitiable than admirable. Even she recognized it as a need in her, growing out of her own nature, rather than a virtue. "I was born under an unlucky star, I suppose," she said. "Now Hida, he's the exact opposite of me."

As one would expect, her considerateness was often a great source of annoyance to her husband, for it was no less irrational and unpredictable than his selfishness. And it had to be said that though a model wife in intention, she was a singularly untalented creature. When young she had been given lessons in the various arts considered necessary to women, but had proved a complete dunce in all of them. She had never learned to sew, for example, and in all the years of their marriage had not made one kimono for her husband.

She was, alas, as willful as she was untalented. Kenzō remembered being told that once, as a child, she had been locked up in the family storehouse as punishment for obstinacy. She had immediately called her mother, and through the barred window insisted that she be let out to urinate or she would do it on the floor where she was standing.

As he recalled the incident he began to wonder whether he was as different from her as he had always believed. "Perhaps," he thought, "she is simply more candid than I am. Without the veneer of education, I might have been very much like her." And he was suddenly convinced that he had for too long placed too much trust in the efficacy of education, that his own learning had done little to alleviate the crudeness of his life. Thus reminded of the essential sameness of people when it came to coping with the harsh realities of day-to-day living, he looked at his sister again and felt a little ashamed of himself.

She had no inkling of his thoughts. "How is Osumi? The baby must be due very soon."

"Yes. She's so huge now, she looks as if she might collapse under the weight any minute."

"It's very hard having a baby—I know."

She had failed to conceive for some years after her marriage. Then, when everybody was beginning to think that she was barren, she had become pregnant. She was rather old to be having her first child, but the delivery had been surprisingly easy. The baby—it was a boy—did not live long, however. "Tell Osumi to be careful," she said. "You know, things would have been easier for us if the boy had lived."

68

SHE was not only mourning her long-dead child; she was suggesting too her dissatisfaction with their adopted son.

"I wish we could depend on Hiko-san more," she said. Perhaps indeed he was not the world's most ambitious man, but the Hiko-san that Kenzō knew was an extremely decent fellow. True, it was rumored that he liked his saké, but at least to someone like Kenzō, who didn't know him too well, he seemed to have no other glaring fault. "It would be a help if he earned a little more money," she continued. No doubt he didn't make enough to enable his foster parents to retire in comfort, but considering the fact that they had never bothered to give him a halfway decent education, they were lucky he earned anything at all.

She bored Kenzō even more when she talked about her dead child. He had never seen the baby, alive or dead. "Let's see, what was his name?"

"Sakutarō, it was," she said, and pointed at the small buddhist shrine on the wall.

It seemed not only appropriately gloomy inside but quite dusty. From where he sat, it was impossible to make out the posthumous names engraved in gold on the black memorial tablets. But he was not going to get up to find out. "I suppose the small one is his."

"That's right. We decided that the normal size wouldn't be quite right for a baby."

His face stayed expressionless. His second daughter had once almost died of dysentery, but not even the memory of his own suffering at the time could make real for him his sister's loss.

She pulled her gaze away from the shrine and said, "At this rate, I might be joining them soon." Kenzō deliberately looked away.

She liked to sound forlorn; here, she was no different from other sick, ageing women. But in fact she did not for a moment believe she was going to die. Her chronic illness might last forever, but so would she.

If nothing else, her obstinacy alone would keep her going. Even when her asthma was at its very worst she would refuse to use the bedpan and would crawl all the way to the toilet; and in the morning, regardless of the weather, she would strip to the waist and rub herself down with cold water. ("I've washed every morning like this since I was a child, and no illness is going to stop me now!")

"You must try to cheer up," said Kenzō, "and take good care of yourself."

"Oh, I take good care of myself, don't you worry. With the pocket money you give me, I make sure always to buy some milk." Peasants believed that eating white rice would cure almost anything; with Kenzō's sister, it was milk.

It struck him as slightly incongruous that he, whose own health was steadily failing, should be expressing such concern for someone else's health. He could not help saying, "I myself am not too well these days. Who knows, I might be joining those tablets sooner than you." She of course thought he was joking, and in self-defense he too laughed as he said this. But he was secretly rather resentful: "She at least can afford to rest when she isn't feeling too well. Here I am, slowly killing myself, and no one cares a damn." With the remnant of his laugh still on his face, he gazed at his sister's emaciated body.

69

*D*ESPITE her naïveté and honesty, there was in her a certain vulgar pettiness which made her at times do things in an unpleasantly circuitous way.

On Kenzō's return to Japan she had come to him with a long woeful account of her economic difficulties; she had then gone to their brother, Chōtarō, and had him ask Kenzō on her behalf if he would send her some pocket money—it didn't matter how much—every month. Kenzō had immediately written back to Chōtarō, specifying the amount he thought he could afford. Then, a few days later, a letter arrived directly from her. Chōtarō had informed her, it said, of the amount; in view of the fact that the money presumably would be sent every month through Chōtarō, would Kenzō now be good enough to let her know in confidence if the amount quoted was right? It was hard to believe, but she was actually doubting Chōtarō's good faith.

The letter was both idiotic and mean—mostly mean. "Shut your mouth!" he felt like shouting. He wrote her only a postcard in reply, but it made clear enough what he thought of her request. There was no further communication from her. She was a near-illiterate, and writing a letter would have been a major undertaking even under more felicitous circumstances.

The incident had made her rather hesitant toward Kenzō; since then, when she was with him, she would manage to curb her normally insatiable curiosity and refrain from asking too personal questions. Kenzō, needless to say, gave her no encouragement. "How is Osumi these days?" would be about all she would dare ask. "As usual, I should say," he would answer, and with that the subject would be dropped.

She was aware, through hearsay, of his wife's past illness, and when she asked about her, she did so as much from kindness as from curiosity. So his dismissal of her tentative inquiries—which he considered useless no matter how well-meant—hurt her and further confirmed her view of him as an unapproachable, insensitive crank.

Kenzō felt quite lonely as he left his sister. He walked vaguely in the direction of his house, knowing that his familiarity with Tokyo geography would get him to his destination eventually. After a while he found himself in a very busy quarter which had that cheap, dirty look peculiar to newly developed areas. There was nothing in the surrounding scene that he could recognize, despite the fact that he had certainly been to this part of Tokyo before. Over the ground from which all vestiges of the past had been taken away, he walked like a man lost.

There had been rice paddies here once, with straight footpaths running between them. Visible on the far side of the paddies were the thatched roofs of farmers' cottages. He could remember seeing a man seated on a bench somewhere around here, his sedge hat beside him, eating jelly. Nearby had stood a large paper mill. One followed the path around the mill and came to a little stream with a bridge over it. The banks were built up high with stones, so that the stream seemed much further below than one had expected. The old-fashioned signs on the bathhouse at the foot of the bridge, the pumpkins lying in front of the grocer's next door—these had often reminded the young Kenzō of Hiroshige's prints.

Now everything was gone like a dream; all that was left was the ground he stood on. "But when did it all go?" He was shocked to see how a place too could change—as though until then he had imagined only people changed.

He had as a child often played chess with Hida. As they were about to start Hida would say, "I, a disciple of the great master, Tōkichi of Tokorozawa, now await your move." Kenzō thought it more than likely that if they were to play now, Hida would still say the same thing.

People really didn't change very much, he thought; they only decayed. They were not like this place, which had not only changed beyond recognition but gained new vigor in the process. As the contrast struck him he could not help wondering: "And what about me? What will I be like in the end?"

70

H*IS* wife immediately noticed his depressed mood when he got home. "How is she?" she asked, obviously certain that the news would be bad. Let's face it, her manner implied, we all have to die some time. Her seriousness struck Kenzō as slightly incongruous under the circumstances. "She's already recovered. She's still in bed, but apart from that, she seems perfectly all right. We were fooled by Chōtarō, I suppose you could say." The whole thing was a farce, he might have added.

"That may well be," she said, "but the important thing is that she's well."

"It wasn't Chōtarō's fault anyway. He was fooled by her. And she in turn was fooled by her own ailment. Well, that's how the world goes—everybody being made a fool of. Hida may actually be the most sensible one of us all. No matter how ill his wife may seem, he's never fooled."

"I don't suppose he was at home?"

"Of course not. Who knows, he might have been there if she had been much worse."

Kenzō was reminded of the imposing gold watch and chain that Hida had somehow acquired and carried about proudly. He led everyone to believe, naturally, that it was solid gold, but Chōtarō insisted behind his back that it must be gold plate and not the real thing. At any rate, no one could discover where he had picked it up or how much he had paid for it. Even Kenzō's sister, with all her inquisitiveness, could only guess. "I'm sure he's paying for it in installments," she would tell Chōtarō without being asked, or, "He may have picked it up in a pawnshop, eh?" The gold watch and chain, which interested Kenzō very little, became for these two the subject of much speculative discussion. Hida, knowing how curious they were, tantalized them by showing off his proud possession as often as he could.

Hida would sometimes take from his wife even the pocket money Kenzō sent her, but presumably he would do so without explanation, for she never had the remotest idea how much he made or how much he had on hand at any given time. She once said to Kenzō in a confidential tone—she might have been talking about the man next door—"I gather he has a few bonds."

A man like Hida, who with such aplomb kept his wife in complete ignorance about his own affairs, was an enigma to Kenzō. So was his sister, who seemed to accept her situation uncomplainingly, as though hers was the lot of any wife. And Kenzō found utterly puzzling, in view of the man's secretiveness, Hida's sudden bursts of open extravagance, when he would come home laden with expensive purchases that left his wife flabbergasted. What was he playing at, Kenzō would wonder; did he simply want to impress her? And why did she not object?

Was it that she did not mind his secretive ways so long as she was occasionally allowed to admire his style? Kenzō had no idea.

He said to his wife, "Money, illness—it doesn't matter what's involved, those two might as well be total strangers. They live in the same house, but that's about all."

His wife, who did not like having to think, had no comment to make.

"But I suppose others think we are a pretty odd couple," he said. "We have no room to talk, maybe."

"Quite right. Everybody thinks he's all right—it's always the other person who's odd."

Kenzō was irritated. "I suppose you think you're all right, then?"

"Certainly. I'm like you in that respect."

It was often in this way that whatever peace of mind they might have been enjoying would be destroyed. They ended up once more thinking the usual unkind thoughts about each other.

"My sister may be illiterate and untalented," Kenzō said, "but she's a devoted wife. On the whole, I rather approve of women like that."

"Anachronisms like that don't grow on every tree these days," she said, thinking what incredibly egocentric creatures men were.

71

F_{OR} a woman lacking in intellectual rigor, Kenzō's wife was surprisingly enlightened. She had grown up in a relaxed home, where strict, old-fashioned standards of conduct were not taken too seriously. Her father, made worldly by life in politics, had no fixed ideas about education, and her mother was unlike most mothers in that she left her daughter more or less alone. After finishing primary school, she had been allowed to roam about the house in comparative freedom.

Her thinking was not complicated, but her ideas were her own, and she adhered to them with primitive tenacity. Her attitude toward Kenzō was typical: "No one is going to force me to respect this man simply because he is my husband. If he wants my respect, he has to show me that he deserves it. His being my husband says nothing about him as a man."

Kenzō, for all his superior education, tended to be more old-fashioned in this respect. He believed sincerely in personal independence and strove hard to realize his ideal; yet shamelessly he assumed that wives existed only to please their husbands: "In all matters, the wife is subordinate to the husband." Herein lay the cause of most of their trouble.

Whenever he was made aware of her desire to assert her existence as a person, he was quick to take offense. "You're only a woman," he would be tempted to say, or, when more than usually annoyed, "Don't be so damned impertinent." Her answer, though unspoken, was clearly written on her face. "I don't care if I'm only a woman, I won't be kicked around." And in the end he would find himself resorting to his wife's argument: "It's not because you're a woman that I consider you stupid—it's because you really are stupid. If you want respect from me, earn it."

And thus they spent their time running around in a circle. How wearying a business it all was they seemed not to know. Occasionally he would come to a halt, and so would she—he to cease for a brief while his agitated shouting, and she to break her tense silence. But even as they talked gently to each other, they remained standing on the circle, ready to start running again.

On coming home from work one evening—it was about ten days before the baby arrived—he learned that his father-in-law had dropped in earlier in the hope of seeing him.

"Was there something he wanted to talk to me about?"

"Apparently."

"What was it?"

She gave no answer.

"Don't you know?"

"No, I don't. He said he'll come again in two or three days, so you can ask him then."

He felt he could not press her any further. But he was curious, and so this time, for a change, he wanted to prolong the conversation. Whatever might have been the inducement, that his father-in-law, whom he himself had not bothered to visit for some time, should have come so far to see him was a total surprise.

His wife, however, was reluctant to pursue the subject. And he could see that her present taciturnity was not touched by resentment or churlishness, as it so often had been before.

That evening winter finally came. The flame of the lamp was steady, but they could hear the wind blowing hard against the storm windows and the trees. They sat in silence, the calmly burning light between them, listening to the harsh sounds of winter outside.

72

"FATHER seemed rather cold without an overcoat," she said. "So I gave him your old one."

It was an inverness cape that Kenzō had had made by a country tailor. It was so old that he had almost forgotten its existence. "That's not the sort of thing you can give anybody," he said, embarrassed. "It's so shabby."

"Not at all. He was very pleased."

"But doesn't he have one of his own?"

"Of course not. For someone in his situation, an overcoat is a luxury."

Kenzō was shocked. He looked at his wife's face in the dim light, and was filled with pity for her. "I didn't know it was that bad."

"He says he's destitute."

In her usual fashion she had said very little to him about her parents' money problems. He knew vaguely that after retirement her father had been hard pressed, but he had never imagined that the man would be penniless.

What a proud figure he used to cut in the mornings, Kenzō thought, as he marched out of his Western-style official residence with its imposing stone gate, in his frock coat and silk hat. The floor of the front hall, Kenzō remembered clearly, was of intricately fitted oak, so beautifully polished that he, unused to such luxury, sometimes slipped on it. The drawing room looked onto a large lawn. Next to it was the dining room, long and narrow. There he had had his first dinner with his fiancée's family. The upstairs was done in the Japanese style, with floor mats in all the rooms. On a cold New Year's night many years ago, he had played cards with the family in one of them. It had been a cozy and cheerful evening.

The residence had a Japanese wing, a sizable house in its own right. The family had in their employ five maids and two student houseboys. True, his father-in-law had to do a great deal of entertaining, and the servants were presumably necessary, but they would not have been there had he not been able to afford them.

Even at the time of Kenzō's return from abroad he had not seemed particularly hard up. Just after Kenzō had moved into the new house he had come over and said this: "It isn't good for a man not to own a house. You can't go on renting forever. Of course, I realize that you're in no position to buy now, and I suppose you'll have to wait. But if I were you, I should start saving right away. House or no house, you should have at least a couple of thousand in the bank, just in case anything happens. As a matter of fact, if you happen to have a thousand to spare, you can give it to me, and within a year I'll make it into two thousand for you."

Being quite unversed in matters of finance, Kenzō had at the time been puzzled as to how one could double one's capital in a year. And not being entirely devoid of greed, he had been much impressed, in fact awestricken, by his father-in-law's seemingly unique talent. But under the circumstances, a million would have made as much sense as a thousand, and he had never bothered to ask how one went about making so much money so quickly.

He said to his wife, "But how could he be so poor?"

"Well, he is, that's all. Just bad luck, you might say."

She was panting. Her physical condition alone was enough of a burden, he thought. Sadly he looked at her belly and then at her sallow, tired face.

Once, shortly after their marriage in the provinces, his father-in-law had come to see them armed with a gift of half a dozen cheap-looking fans. On each was painted an ukiyoe-type beauty. Twirling one of them around in his fingers Kenzō had remarked, "Rather vulgar, aren't they sir?" "Yes, but quite suited to this household," had been the quick retort.

The overcoat had been made about that time, in the same provincial town. He could hardly say to the old gentleman now, he thought wryly, "Shabby, yes, but quite suited to its wearer."

The pathos of the situation drove him almost to exasperation. "But how could he think of wearing it," he said.

His wife smiled: "I suppose he'd rather be shabby than cold."

73

TWO days later Kenzō's father-in-law came again, and this time Kenzō was at home. The two had not seen each other for a long time.

Not only because of his age but because of the kind of life he had led, he was a far worldlier and more tactful man than Kenzō. He treated his son-in-law always with politeness; indeed, his manner was sometimes almost too careful. But underneath the surface politeness, there lurked a certain animosity and resentment.

To this man whose character had been formed in the world of officials, Kenzō had seemed from the first impudent, always too prone to ignore protocol. Moreover, he found unpleasant Kenzō's obvious conceit, his blatant opinionatedness. And he found more ill-mannered than honest Kenzō's habit of saying exactly what he thought. In short, he believed he had a boor for a son-in-law.

Contemptuous of what he believed to be Kenzō's basic puerility, he had discouraged with cold politeness the younger man's innocent and crude efforts to come close to him. And there the two had stopped; now all either could do was to look at the other over the gulf, suspicious and disapproving, unaware of most of his own failings and of the other's virtues.

Today the old man was clearly at a disadvantage. Pressed for money, he had had to come to his son-in-law for help. Kenzō, who hated to beg for anything from anybody, could not help asking himself how he would have felt had he been put in the other's place. "It must be terrible for him," he kept on thinking.

But it was impossible for him even to pretend friendliness as he listened. And cursing his own inability to dissemble, he wanted desperately to explain: "It isn't because money is involved that I seem so unfriendly—it isn't the talk of money that I find painful. Please understand, I'm not so base as to think of this as an opportunity for revenge." But his nature being what it was, he had to remain silent and run the risk of being misunderstood.

There was no such clumsiness, social ineptness, in his father-in-law. He was his usual polite and controlled self. An onlooker would have had no trouble deciding which of the two was more the gentleman. He mentioned a certain person, then said, "This man says he knows you. Do you know him?"

"Yes, I do." Kenzō had known him at the university, but they had never been close. After graduation the man had gone to Germany. On his return he had decided not to remain in his profession and gone to work in a bank. But this had been some time ago, and Kenzō had heard nothing since about him. "Is he still in the bank?" he asked. His father-in-law nodded. Kenzō had no idea how the two might have met. But there seemed to be no point in asking; after all, the main question was whether or not this old acquaintance of Kenzō's would lend the money.

"At any rate, what he says is that he will lend me the money if I can find a reliable guarantor."

"I see."

"When I asked whom he might accept, he specifically mentioned you."

Kenzō had no doubt at all about his own reliability. But anyone who knew what he did for a living must also know that he couldn't possibly have much money to spare. Besides, his father-in-law had a wide circle of acquaintances, and among those he was in the habit of mentioning, there were many famous men who would have been regarded by the world at large as far better risks than Kenzō.

"But why does he want me?"

"He says he will lend it if you're the guarantor."

Kenzō became thoughtful.

74

KENZŌ had never in his life borrowed money from a source which required a formal guarantee. But unknowledgable though he was about such matters, he had at least heard about able men who were now in desperate straits, whose careers had been irrevocably ruined, because they had backed other men's debts. And he felt that he should at all costs avoid getting involved in anything that might put him in such a predicament. The trouble with him, however, was that behind the obstinacy there was a rather indecisive streak in his character. He simply did not have the courage to refuse outright to lend his signature; he was afraid of seeming too heartless.

"Must it be me?" he asked again, and got the same reply: "He says he'll lend it to me if you're the guarantor." "How odd," he said innocently, not being able to guess, as anyone more worldly would have done immediately, that his father-in-law had come to him simply because everyone else had refused. Naïvely he began to feel a little frightened by the amount of trust the banker, whom he had never known very well, seemed to have in him.

"Be careful, don't do anything stupid. . . ." His immediate reaction was to avoid danger, to protect himself. But he was not simple enough to act spontaneously even in his own interest; he had to continue to vacillate until he had worked out in his head a feasible solution. And even when such a solution did finally present itself, he had to force himself to suggest it to his father-in-law.

"I really don't want to sign any papers," he said. "It's too dangerous. However, I'll try to raise whatever money I can on my own. Of course, I have no savings, so it means I shall have to borrow it. But I am going to try a friend first; that way, I don't have to get involved in unpleasant formalities. I'd feel a lot safer, and altogether happier. Needless to say, I am not going to be able to raise anything like the sum you mentioned. Since I'm doing the borrowing, I can only borrow what is within my ability to pay back."

Kenzō's father-in-law was in no position to object. He was so poor, he had to receive gratefully whatever was offered him. "I'm much obliged to you," he said. He put on Kenzō's old overcoat and walked out into the cold winter sunlight.

The two men had done their talking in the study. Without looking at his wife who stood beside him in the front hall, Kenzō now went straight back there. She did not follow him. She knew what her father had come about, and Kenzō knew that she knew. But neither seemed to want to bring the subject up.

Kenzō had accepted yet another responsibility. He had no time to lose; on that very same day he went to see his eccentric friend, the one who had helped him buy the household furnishings.

Without preamble Kenzō blurted out, "How about lending me some money." His friend, who never had much cash on him, was momentarily stunned. Warming his cold hands over the brazier Kenzō explained the situation in detail. "Well," he said, "can you do anything?"

He had managed to save a little, his friend said, during the three years he taught in China, but he had invested all of it in a railroad. "In that case," Kenzō persisted, "what about Shimizu?" Shimizu was his friend's brother-in-law. He was a doctor, and ran a private hospital in one of the busier sections downtown.

"I really don't know," his friend said. "He should have some money, but it may be all tied up. I'll ask and see."

And so, thanks to his friend's goodwill, Kenzō managed to raise four hundred yen. Four or five days later it was in his father-in-law's hands.

75

"I'VE done all I can," he said to himself. He was so relieved that he gave no thought to the amount of money he had been able to raise. He expected no gratitude from his father-in-law; neither did he wonder what so little would do for him. And he was quite content to remain ignorant as to what uses the money would be put to. His father-in-law for his part seemed equally content to keep his private affairs to himself.

The incident was perhaps too inconsequential in itself to help close the gap between them. Or perhaps the two men were too set in their ways to change.

His father-in-law valued worldly success, and thus the opinion of others, more than Kenzō did. Whether or not others really understood him concerned him little; what was of greater importance to him was that he should impress them. Consequently, in his behavior toward his relatives, there was more than a touch of self-importance.

When circumstances took a sudden turn for the worse, he was forced to question his past behavior. This made him all the more defensive, and in Kenzō's presence he tried hard to pretend that all was still well with him. It was out of sheer desperation that he had finally come to Kenzō for help. But even then he did not deign to explain how desperate he really was. And Kenzō did not ask.

They had briefly stretched out their hands, one man to give and the other to take, then had immediately withdrawn them. Kenzō's wife stood on the side, watching the impersonal transaction and saying nothing.

At the time of Kenzō's return from abroad, the two men were not so distant from each other. It was not long after Kenzō and his family had moved into their new house that his father-in-law became interested in a mining enterprise.

"Mining?" Kenzō remembered saying to his wife in surprise.

"That's right. He's going to set up a company."

Kenzō frowned. But in those days he was still in awe of what he believed to be his father-in-law's phenomenal ability. "I suppose it will be all right?" he said, wanting to be reassured.

"I hope so," she said.

Soon after Kenzō received word that his father-in-law had left for a city in the north. Then about a week later his mother-in-law appeared at his house. Her husband had suddenly fallen ill, she said; she had to go to him, but she couldn't afford the fare; would Kenzō help her?

"Of course," Kenzō said, feeling deeply sorry for the poor lady about to journey all alone to the gray, distant north that he himself had never seen, and for his father-in-law whom he pictured lying helplessly in a strange bed. "You must go at once."

"All I got was a short telegram, so I have no way of knowing what's really the matter with him."

"That must be very worrying. You should leave as soon as you can."

Fortunately his father-in-law's illness was not serious. As for the mining company, Kenzō heard no more about it. "Can't your father find a suitable post?" he asked his wife a little later.

"Apparently there are possibilities," she said, "but so far nothing has quite worked out." She then went on to tell him about the time her father had been put up as a candidate for mayor of a certain large city. An old friend was to have provided the necessary campaign funds. Then a group of prominent men of that city had come up to Tokyo to consult a famous politician—he was a count—concerning her father's qualifications for the office. "He won't do," the count had said, and that was the end of her father's candidacy.

"It can't go on like this," Kenzō said.

"Don't worry," his wife answered. "Something will turn up."

She had far greater confidence in her father than Kenzō did. Kenzō too had not yet lost his naïve admiration for men of affairs. "I'm worried for his sake, not mine," he said, quite truthfully.

76

*B*UT when Kenzō's father-in-law came to the house after his return from the north, the relationship between the two men had undergone a change. The younger man who had offered to lend the fare was now obliged to step back and view his senior from a distance. One would have said that Kenzō's manner betrayed a cold indifference. But what he really felt was animosity; the indifference was merely a cover.

His father-in-law was in a near-desperate situation. Yet to everyone around him, he remained as always ostentatiously polite. Repelled by the politeness and unable to approach him with any open sympathy, Kenzō in turn became defensive, and his natural goodwill was transformed into a kind of boorishness; and he found himself hating the other's misfortune and politeness.

No doubt his father-in-law found Kenzō's manner unbearably insulting; after all, it was improper for anyone to behave thus, let alone a junior. An outside observer, knowing nothing of the circumstances, would have considered Kenzō's behavior simply stupid. Even his wife, if asked, would hardly have called it intelligent.

"This time, I'm in real trouble," his father-in-law said. Seeing that Kenzō was not about to say anything, he proceeded to mention the name of a famous financier. "Someone was good enough to give me an introduction to him. It looks as though he may be able to arrange something for me. As you know, his combine is second only to Mitsui and Mitsubishi, so being one of his hired men won't be altogether undignified. Besides, one can do all kinds of interesting things in a large concern like that."

He had been promised, he said, the managing directorship of a railway company in the west. The financier owned most of the shares, so that he could appoint anyone he liked to the position.

Surely, Kenzō thought, his father-in-law would be expected to own a few shares, but where would he find the money to buy them? As though reading his mind, his father-in-law quickly added, "He is going to transfer the necessary number of shares to me for the time being." Kenzō did not have so low an opinion of his ability or his general reputation as to be skeptical. Besides, for both selfish and unselfish reasons, he wanted to believe that his father-in-law's troubles would soon be over. But for all his goodwill, he could not change his manner. "I am happy to hear that," he said coldly, taking care to stifle the sympathy he felt tentatively growing within himself.

The old veteran showed no sign of resentment. "The trouble is," he said calmly, "I can't hurry him. That would be unwise." He pulled out of his pocket an imposing document and showed it to Kenzō. It was a letter of contract from an insurance company, stating that he had been appointed a part-time consultant with a monthly honorarium of a hundred yen. "I don't know whether I shall continue with this when the other matter is settled, but even a hundred yen a month is something I can't ignore at the moment."

This same man, Kenzō thought, had once indignantly turned down an offer of a provincial governorship. The offer had been a conciliatory gesture on the part of his superiors, who had forced him to resign his post in the central government. That he should now accept with equanimity a measly hundred yen a month from an insurance company, and not a particularly thriving one at that, showed how much circumstances had changed him.

Such frankness from his father-in-law almost disarmed Kenzō. But when he felt his heart softening, he quickly put up his defenses again. Others might consider his defensiveness abnormal, but he knew intuitively that his behavior was morally justified.

All this, then, had already happened when the overcoat was given.

77

KENZŌ'S father-in-law was a practical man. And he tended to evaluate other men solely in terms of their success in their jobs. When General Nogi, for example, resigned his post as viceroy of Formosa after a very short tour of duty, he had made this comment to Kenzō: "The general is a man of honor and feeling, I know, and I admire him as a person. But the question is, was he the right man for the viceroyship? A man's private virtues may benefit those who come into direct contact with him, but what about all those millions of subjects whom he never sees? Practical ability—that's the important thing. Without it, a man, no matter how virtuous, is helpless."

Once, when still in office, he had managed the business affairs of a certain society which had as its president a marquis. When the work of the society was accomplished, thanks largely to his efforts, surplus funds amounting to about twenty thousand yen were entrusted to him. However, when his official career came to an untimely end and there followed a long period of financial hardship, he could not resist laying his hands on the money. Soon it was all gone. Fearful of losing the confidence of his family, he said nothing about it to them at the time. And secretly, in order to save his reputation, he scraped up every month the amount equivalent to the interest that the money would have fetched, which was roughly a hundred yen.

This obligation, then, had troubled him more than the responsibility of feeding his family. That he could now get from the insurance company the hundred yen a month, so necessary to the continuation of his public life, must have been an enormous relief to him.

Kenzō's wife had eventually learned what her father had done and had told him about it. His inward response had been totally sympathetic, not in the slightest indignant or contemptuous. And he had felt no shame whatsoever in being married to the daughter of what others might call an embezzler. Neither had he deemed it necessary to tell her so.

She would on occasion say something like this: "I don't care what kind of a man I'm married to, so long as he treats me decently." "What if I were a thief?" "I wouldn't care. A thief, a swindler, or anything you like. All a wife wants is a considerate husband. Kindness at home is what I want. I can't live on your distinction or rectitude, you know."

While agreeing with what she said—and he knew she was being honest—he would wonder whether her comments were not an oblique way of saying that he should spend more time with his family and less time with his books. But what really bothered him was the thought that perhaps she, ignorant of his true sentiments, was trying to defend her father. And while making no effort to explain himself to her, he found it necessary to tell himself over and over again, "What he did has nothing to do with the way I feel about him—I'm not like that at all."

It was his father-in-law's vain punctiliousness, Kenzō insisted to himself, that had brought about their estrangement.

There was the incident of the previous New Year. Kenzō

had not bothered to go to his father-in-law's house to pay his respects; instead, he had sent a card with the conventional greetings on it. His father-in-law was clearly annoyed, and he showed his annoyance in a characteristic fashion. He had his youngest daughter, just turned twelve, scrawl "Happy New Year" on a card, then had her send it to Kenzō in her name. He was a man who knew how to retaliate without being coarse; yet for all his social adeptness, he never thought to ask himself why it was that Kenzō had not come to see him.

It was only a little incident in itself, but it was given significance by all that had happened before, and it set the two men yet further apart.

Kenzō saw a great difference between a man who offends because he is forced to and a man who hurts others unnecessarily and deliberately. He now began to hate his father-in-law with all his heart for his calculated ways.

78

KENZŌ was willing enough to recognize that there was a naïve side to himself, that he could quite easily be taken advantage of. That others might think so too, however, made him cross.

There were people who accepted the fact of their own naïveté or credulousness and seemed not to mind if others knew it. Kenzō could always pick such people out in a crowd. He was instinctively drawn to them, and felt an almost violent longing to know them. That he could never be like them made him admire them all the more.

Yet he was inconsistent enough to hate himself for what he believed to be his weakness, and he hated even more those who made him hate himself.

Thus the gulf between him and his father-in-law continued to widen. His wife's attitude toward him, alas, did nothing to check the process.

Again, whenever relations between him and his wife became strained, she would look to her parents for sympathy, and they would then be given no choice but to take her side. And sometimes, being her allies necessarily meant that they were his enemies. In the end, her going to them only made the situation worse for her and Kenzō.

Fortunately there was always her hysteria to bring harmony back to the couple. Her attacks seemed invariably to come just when the tension between them had reached the maximum point. One night Kenzō found her lying face down in the middle of the verandah leading to the toilet. Another night he found her crouched precariously on the edge of the same verandah, by an open storm window. Kenzō put his arms around her waist from behind, pulled her up, then gently took her back to bed.

There was hardly any awareness in her at such times. Reality and dream were indistinguishable to her then. Her eyes were wide open, the pupils enlarged, and Kenzō guessed that what they saw was a phantom world.

He would sit at her bedside for a while, with fear in his heart. Sometimes he would be filled with compassion. He would comb her pitifully disarranged hair or wipe the sweat off her forehead with a wet towel. On occasion, to bring her to, he would blow water on her face, or bring his mouth to hers and make her swallow some.

He would remember too the old days when her attacks were more severe, and grow frightened.

In those days, he had frequently tied one end of a string to her sash and the other end to his to make sure she could not go any-where without his knowing. The string was long enough to allow them to turn over in bed without waking each other. She had never objected to this device, even after it had been repeated many nights running. Once, during a fit, he had had to place the bottom of a rice bowl flat on the pit of her stomach, then push with all his might until her taut body, unbelievably resistant, had finally relaxed. She had also said some very strange things: "Look, look, there's the divine messenger, come to visit us on his five-colored cloud!" "Let me go, let me go! The dead baby's come back, and I've got to go. Can't you see, he's there, waiting for me in the bucket!" This had been a few days after a mis-carriage.

The fits nowadays were not so severe. But they still upset Kenzō. Most times when she was ill he felt great affection and pity for her. He treated her as gently as he could, as though she were some helpless, fragile creature, and she seemed pleased and grateful.

Therefore, so long as he did not think her attacks feigned, so long as he did not lose his temper at her antics, and so long as the frequency of the attacks did not finally exhaust his supply of sympathy and begin to make him feel victimized, her hysteria was essential to Kenzō as a means of bringing him closer to his wife.

Unfortunately no such convenient pacifying agent was available to him and his father-in-law. Their estrangement had originally come about on account of Kenzō's wife, but it had by now become an independent phenomenon, hardly likely to disappear simply because her marriage for the time being was working out well. It was a perverse sort of situation perhaps, but nonetheless very real.

79

*T*HE animosity between him and his father-in-law was indeed senseless, and it distressed him. Nevertheless he accepted it. He was not without a certain stubborn single-mindedness, but there was also in his character more than a touch of passivity, of defeatism. "It's not up to me to do anything about it," he told himself with finality, quite convinced that the mutual animosity would never lessen; as far as he was concerned, it was a permanent condition of their relationship.

Unfortunately his wife was equally reluctant to take a positive stand in the matter. It was not that she was constitutionally incapable of action. Indeed, when faced with some concrete problem, she could act with a decisiveness that would have done many men proud. But the problem had to present itself as a particular incident, as an event that needed immediate practical attention; otherwise she refused to deal with it. For her, then, her relationship with Kenzō was too nebulous a thing to be recognized as a problem; so was the animosity between her husband and her father. As long as the two men did not engage in open warfare, as long as they kept their frustrations inside themselves, she would stand aside and do nothing.

"But nothing really has happened between you two," she persisted in saying, and she believed what she said. According to her standards, nothing had indeed happened. What her eyes did not see, what she could not point her finger at, was not an "event." Sometimes Kenzō would look at her accusingly, as though she were some kind of liar, but this made her all the more set in her passivity.

Such passivity, then, or fatalism if you will, was one characteristic Kenzō and his wife had in common. Others might say that they were perversely trying to perpetuate a state of disharmony between themselves. But in fact the unhappy situation was no more controllable than their own stubborn characters. They would look at each other's face and conduct themselves in accordance with what they thought they saw. It did not occur to either to try to change the other's supposed frame of mind.

After Kenzō's father-in-law had left their house with the money, the two saw fit not to talk about him.

"When does the midwife say the baby is due?"

"She hasn't said yet. All I know is that it will be very soon."

"Have all the preparations been made?"

"Oh yes, everything is in the closet in the bedroom."

Kenzō had no idea what had been put in the closet.

She sighed heavily and said, "I can't go on much longer like this—it's so uncomfortable. I hope it will be very soon."

"I shouldn't be in such a hurry if I were you. After all, you did say you might die this time."

"I don't care. All I want is to be rid of this terrible weight."

"I *am* sorry," he said, lightly.

He remembered the time their eldest child was born in the provinces. He had been hovering about uneasily in the next room when the midwife asked him to come in and help her. As soon as he sat down his wife had grabbed his hand and held it with such force that he thought his bones would break. She had groaned terribly too, like someone under torture. He had sat helplessly by, feeling hurt and guilty.

"It's no fun for someone watching either," he now said.

"Well then, go out somewhere and amuse yourself."

"Do you think you can manage by yourself?"

She said nothing—not even that she had after all given birth to her second child while he was thousands of miles away. And he was careful not to ask her how she had managed then; he didn't want to know.

He was a big worrier, and he was hardly the man to leave a groaning wife behind and nonchalantly wander about the streets in search of entertainment.

When the midwife next called he made a point of asking her, "When will it be? Within a week, would you say?"

"No," she said, "it will be later."

Both Kenzō and his wife assumed she was right.

80

BUT her time came much sooner than expected. One night Kenzō was awakened from a deep sleep by his wife. She was obviously in great pain. "It began hurting a little while ago," she managed to say.

"Is it about to come out?" he asked, poking his head out from under the bedclothes. It was a very cold night. "Would you like me to massage you?" He didn't want to get out of bed, and he hoped that a mere voicing of good intentions would be sufficient.

He wondered exactly how bad her pain was. He had witnessed a delivery only once, and whatever he might have learned then was now mostly forgotten. But he thought he could remember that such pains had come and gone many times before the child was born. "I shouldn't worry," he said. "If you wait a minute, I'm sure the pain will go away."

"All I know is that it's getting worse and worse." There was no doubt about it, she was truly suffering. Her head, rolling now to the right and now to the left with each new wave of pain, had fallen off the pillow.

"Shall I call the midwife?"

"Yes, and please hurry."

The midwife, as might be expected of someone in her calling, had a telephone in her house. But his was hardly the kind of household that would be equipped with such useful, up-to-date items. Whenever there was a need to use the telephone, they simply went to the local doctor's house and used his.

It was a dark winter night, and dawn was yet some hours away. He did not relish the thought of sending the maid out into the cold and waking the poor doctor up in the middle of the night, but he could not afford to wait till morning. His mind made up, he rushed to the maid's room at the other end of the house and sent her scurrying into the dark night.

When he got back to his wife, her pain had grown much worse. He sat down beside her and waited with tense impatience for the sound of an approaching rickshaw.

The night's silence was now being ceaselessly broken by his wife's groans. Then—perhaps no more than five minutes had passed—she looked at him and said, "It's coming." She let out a loud cry, as though she had tried but could no longer hold it in, and the baby was born.

"Don't worry," he said, "it'll be all right," and quickly moved to the foot of her bed. He did not know what to do.

Through its narrow chimney the lamp gave out a faint, still glow, reminiscent somehow of death. He looked around the room, and all he saw was shadows. He could not even make out the bold stripes on the bedding. He was utterly confused.

He knew he should bring the lamp close so that he could see what he was doing. But he felt that a man should not see what was there. He reached out in the near-darkness and touched an object the like of which he had never felt before. It was firm, yet yielding. And it had no recognizable shape. With some revulsion he stroked the shapeless lump. It neither moved nor made a sound. He thought—he was not sure—that every time he passed his fingers over it, some of the jelly-like substance peeled off. Suddenly afraid that it might crumble under the slightest pressure, he withdrew his hand.

Then he began to worry that if he did nothing for this still, silent creature, it might catch cold or even freeze to death. He now remembered his wife mentioning the closet. He went to it, slid open the door, and got out a roll of material—he did not even know that it was called absorbent cotton. Tearing it into little pieces, he piled the stuff over the unprotesting lump.

81

*T*HE midwife came at last, and with a sigh of relief Kenzō retired to his own room.

Soon it was light outside. The baby's cries shook the cold air in the house.

"It was a safe delivery," the midwife said to Kenzō. "Congratulations."

"Is it a boy or a girl?"

"A girl," said the midwife, looking at him sympathetically.

He did not hide his disappointment. "So it's another girl."

He was now the father of three girls. What did his wife think she was doing, he thought bitterly, completely ignoring the fact that she hadn't exactly made them herself.

His first daughter, born in the provinces, had been a pretty baby with delicate features. He had enjoyed taking her out into the streets in the baby carriage. And he would walk home gazing at the angelic little face in slumber. But alas, time will always destroy vain hopes. The girl who came out to Shimbashi Station to meet her father on his return from abroad had said to someone beside her, "He isn't much to look at, is he." That was precisely his reaction when he saw her. Her looks had decidedly changed for the worse during his absence; her face had become more pinched-looking, her features more angular. And he was forced to admit that she had after all inherited his own worst features.

His second daughter's head was always covered with boils. Her hair had been chopped off mercilessly to allow more air through. She had a small chin and big eyes, and the total effect was rather bizarre. Kenzō would occasionally find her wandering about the house looking a little lost, like some visitor from monster-land.

That his third daughter might grow up to be a decent-looking person was somehow beyond hope. "One ugly child after another, and to what end?" Often such a thought, not very proper in a father, entered his mind. And of course it expressed his hopelessness not only as a father but as a husband too.

He looked in on his wife on his way out. She lay peacefully between clean sheets. The baby had been wrapped in new bedclothes and placed beside her, like some appurtenance. It had a red face and bore no resemblance at all to the shapeless, jelly-like creature he had touched in the night.

The room was altogether orderly and clean, with not a soiled thing in sight. What had happened during the night now seemed a dream.

"You've given her a new mattress," he said to the midwife.

"Yes, and fresh sheets."

"It's a wonder you managed to clean the room up so quickly."

The midwife merely smiled. She was a spinster, and there was about her manner a touch of masculinity. "You left me hardly any absorbent cotton."

"Well, I was desperate," he said without apology. He turned to his wife and looked worriedly at her bloodless face. "How do you feel?"

She opened her eyes a little and gave a slight nod. Kenzō left without saying any more.

When he returned that evening he went straight to his wife without changing into Japanese clothes. "How do you feel?" he asked again.

This time she said, "Something's wrong." Her face was flushed with fever.

"You don't feel well?"

"No."

"Shall I get the midwife?"

"There's no need," she said. "She's already been called."

82

*T*HE midwife looked at the thermometer, then shook the mercury down. "She does have a slight fever." She was a woman of few words. Without even discussing the advisability of calling an obstetrician, she went home.

"Is it all right to leave it like this?" Kenzō asked his wife.

"I suppose."

He felt helpless and ignorant. He had heard ominous things about childbed fever, and he began to wonder fearfully if that was what she had. Of the two, she was certainly the more confident, partly because she had faith in the midwife whom she had inherited from her mother.

"What do you mean, 'I suppose'?" he said crossly. "It's your body you're talking about, you know."

She said nothing. He looked suspiciously at her face: is she saying she doesn't care what happens to her?

The next morning as he left for work he was still resenting her casualness. "Why should I worry when she herself is so offhand?"

When he returned her temperature had gone down to normal. "So it was nothing after all," he said.

"That's right. Mind you, there's no telling when the fever will come back."

"Does one's temperature always go up and down like that after one's had a baby? I had no idea."

She looked at her husband's solemn face and smiled sadly.

The fever fortunately never came back, and there were no further complications. During the three weeks that she had to remain in bed, he sat often at her bedside and talked to her.

"Here you are, lying quite comfortably," he once said to her. "You were going to die this time, remember?"

"If you want me to, I'll die any time you say."

"Go ahead, no one's stopping you."

She could joke about it now, but she really had had a premonition, dim though it might have been. "I did think I was going to die."

"Why?"

"I don't know—I just did."

She seemed to accept with perfect aplomb the fact that contrary to her expectations she had had an unusually easy delivery. "How casual you can be sometimes," he said.

"You're the casual one," she said, and looked happily at the baby sleeping beside her. She then poked its little cheek and made cooing noises. The baby's face was quite unformed, and looked hardly human to Kenzō.

"No wonder you had an easy time," he said. "It's terribly tiny."

"Don't worry, she'll get bigger."

This small lump of flesh, Kenzō thought, will one day grow up to be a woman, like my wife. Of course, that was very far away in the future, but barring death, it was bound to happen. "What a drawn-out and difficult thing it is," he said, "to complete anything in one's life."

"What in the world are you talking about?" she said, somewhat shaken.

"You heard what I said."

"Well, what did you mean by it?"

"Nothing. I meant no more than what I said."

"Please yourself then. You get a lot of satisfaction out of saying things other people don't understand, don't you?" She turned to her baby again and drew it close to her. She had dismissed her husband. Without resentment he got up and went to his study.

He was thinking not only of his wife, who had not died, and the healthy baby, but of his brother, who expected any day to lose his job, yet was managing to hold onto it; of his asthmatic sister, who had somehow kept death at bay; of his father-in-law, who seemed always to be on the verge of finding new employment; and of Shimada and Otsune. And he wondered when his relationship with all these people would ever reach a point of completion.

83

*T*HE happiest were the two little girls. A live doll had been unexpectedly presented to them, and whenever they could, they played with it. They marveled at the way it blinked; they stared in fascination as it sneezed or yawned. Conscious only of the immediate present, they never thought that they themselves might grow and acquire new ways; so that every new movement the baby made, everything it had not done before was a source of enormous surprise.

In their preoccupation with the present, they were even further removed from Kenzō than from their mother. Sometimes, when he got home, he would look in on the family before changing his clothes. He would gaze at the happy group of mother and her three children, then think to himself, "A jolly foursome again, I see," and stalk out. Sometimes he would elect to join the group, and make an attempt at asserting his authority, much to his wife's amusement. "What, another hot water bottle for the baby?" he would say, pretending to know what he was talking about. "Don't you know it's very unhealthy? How many hot water bottles have you already put in the bed, anyway?"

Many days had passed since the baby was born, but he had not once held it in his arms. In spite of this, he would exhibit a certain possessiveness when he saw the family together.

He said to his wife one day, "I suppose it's natural for a woman to want her children all to herself."

She stared up at him from her bed in surprise. Kenzō thought he detected a look of guilt too, as though she had been told something about herself that she had chosen to ignore. "What made you say that all of a sudden?" she said.

"But it's true. Isn't that how a dissatisfied wife often strikes back at her husband?"

"Don't be a fool. If they prefer me, it's because you won't let them come near you."

"And who is responsible for that?"

"All right, say anything you please. You're warped, that's your trouble. And so clever with words too."

Kenzō really believed what he was saying. He was not consciously being perverse. He said, "What I don't like about women is that they're born schemers."

She turned her head away. She was crying. "Why do you have to be so cruel?"

The children, who had been watching all along, now looked as though they too might start crying. Feeling oppressed and helpless in the face of such display of weakness, he began to apologize. But he remained convinced that what he had said was right; the tears that he wiped away from his wife's face had no effect on his way of thinking.

At their next encounter, she began immediately to attack him where he was most vulnerable. "Why have you never held the baby?"

"It's not safe, that's why," he said feebly. "I wouldn't want to break its neck, you know."

"Stop lying. I'll tell you why—it's because you don't care enough about your wife or your children."

"But it's so limp. How can a clumsy man like me hold it and be sure he won't hurt it?"

The baby did indeed look as though it had no bones. But his wife was not persuaded. She reminded him of the time their oldest daughter had caught chicken pox. "Your attitude toward her changed overnight, remember? Until then, you doted on her. But after that, you refused to let her come anywhere near you."

She was telling the truth, and he knew it, but his self-righteousness was quite unshaken. He walked away, firmly convinced that women were tricky creatures and that it was pointless arguing with them. He did not imagine for a moment that he might at times appear rather tricky too.

84

*H*AVING nothing to do all day, Kenzō's wife began taking novels out of the lending library. He once said to her, eyeing the shabby, paper-covered volume lying by her bed, "Do you really enjoy reading stuff like that?"

She had been reminded too often of how different she and Kenzō were to tolerate such a remark from him. "Yes I do, even if you don't. What I read is my own business, don't you think?"

She had known very few men before her marriage: her father, her brother, and two or three of her father's colleagues. And from this rather limited sampling she had formed a general preconception about men. After her marriage, she had discovered to her surprise that what her husband wanted from life was not at all like what these others—especially her father—had wanted. Simplemindedly she had then decided that since Kenzō and her father could not both be right, obviously Kenzō was wrong. But the certainty that with experience Kenzō would one day grow to be like her father had given her comfort for a little while.

Alas, Kenzō had proved no less unalterable than herself. It was inevitable, therefore, that they should have come to hold each other in contempt. Always ready to judge by her father's standards, she found many of her husband's ways hard to stomach. Kenzō in turn hated her for her unwillingness to give him the recognition he felt he deserved. And being rash, he would sometimes punish her by flaunting his superiority.

"If you think me stupid for reading this sort of thing," she continued, "why not do something about it? Teach me, instead of insulting me."

"You've no intention of learning anything from me, that's why. One can't educate the ineducable, as they say."

What fool would sit at your feet, was her thought.

They had said more or less the same things to each other many times before. And the oftener they repeated themselves, the more reluctant they became to change their views.

Tired of arguing, Kenzō threw down the book he had picked up for a cursory look. "I am not saying you shouldn't read it. You read whatever you want. But you must be careful not to tire your eyes."

Sewing was her favorite recreation. When she couldn't go to sleep, for example, she would sit by the lamp and sew until one or two o'clock in the morning. She had once strained her eyes very badly by starting to sew too soon after one of the older girls had been born. She had of course been more youthful then, more recklessly confident of her own stamina.

"Yes, I'll be careful," she said. "But reading isn't as harmful as sewing. Besides, I don't read all the time."

"Don't go on reading until you get tired, that's all I ask. You'll regret it later if you do."

"Don't fuss." She was not yet thirty, and having little idea of what it meant to overexert oneself, she refused to take her husband seriously.

"All right, if you can't think of your own welfare, at least think of mine." It was his habit to say something blatantly selfish when he felt his wife was ignoring him. It was another of his features she found unattractive.

He went back to his study to continue his scribbling. His handwriting, which had for some time been very small, was now even smaller; the characters looked more than ever like rows of little ants crawling up and down the page. That they were perhaps illegible was of no great concern, however, for he did not really know exactly what he was writing down with such fervor. At dusk, when there was hardly any light coming in through the window, and late at night by the feebly glowing lamp, he scribbled and scribbled. At last exhausted, he crawled out of the study, his eyes bloodshot and half blind. He had that very day cautioned his wife about her eyes, but neither he nor she seemed to see anything inconsistent in his behavior.

85

*B*Y the time his wife was allowed to leave her bed, winter had completed its work on their garden. Looking at the barren scene that was decorated only by ice columns, she said, "What an unusually cold winter it is."

"You think so because you lost blood."

"Maybe you're right," she said. "I hadn't thought of that." She brought her hands away from the brazier and looked at her colorless fingernails.

"Can't you tell when you look at yourself in the mirror?"

"Of course," she said, putting her hands on her pale cheeks. "But it's cold weather we're having all the same."

Kenzō was amused at her refusal to listen to his explanation. "It's bound to be cold—what else do you expect in the middle of winter?"

For all his brave talk he himself was more affected by the cold than most, and it seemed to him that this winter was particularly bad. He had indeed been forced to have a large foot warmer and a coverlet brought into his study so that at least the lower part of his body would not freeze. He did not suspect that his increased sensitivity to the cold might be in part due to his mental condition. In that he could at times be lacking in self-awareness, he was no different from his wife.

It was her custom to complete her morning toilet after she had seen her husband off to work. That morning again she sat forlornly before the mirror, gazing at all the hair that had come out with the combing. Losing blood at childbirth had not affected her half so much. Every time I bear a child, I give a part of myself away—such was her feeling. It remained vague in her mind, for she was not used to articulating her feelings. Yet no matter how faintly recognized, it brought with it a sense of accomplishment, and at the same time resentment. Either way, it increased her love for the newborn child.

That evening Kenzō watched her pick up the limp, rubber-like baby with impressive ease and kiss its round cheek. What has come out of my body is mine by right, she seemed to be saying.

She returned to her sewing. From time to time she would stop and look concernedly at the baby sleeping comfortably beside her.

"Whose kimono are you making?" he asked.

"The baby's."

"Another one?"

"Yes," she said, and kept on sewing.

He looked at the brightly colored cloth on her lap. "A present from my sister, I suppose?"

"That's right."

"Why does she have to do it? She simply can't afford to give presents like that." He was quite genuinely at a loss to understand his sister's motives. "She obviously had to spend a part of the pocket money I sent her to buy that. She was spending my money, in fact."

"She did it because she felt she should. She was under an obligation to you, she would say."

True enough, his sister was one of those women who lost all sense of proportion where obligations were concerned. For every gift received, she would starve in order to give back something much better. "Why won't she ever learn? Why doesn't she forget about these silly little conventions and do something sensible for a change, like making sure her husband doesn't steal any of her money?"

What other people did to satisfy their whims was of no concern to Kenzō's wife. She said with characteristic indifference, "I'll give her something next time I see her, so don't worry."

Giving people presents was not one of Kenzō's habits. He continued to stare suspiciously at the piece of muslin in his wife's lap.

86

"APPARENTLY people would force presents on her for that reason," his wife said suddenly. "Whatever they gave her, they knew she would give back something that cost half as much again."

"So they would spend fifty sen and she seventy-five sen—it's hardly worth talking about."

"But perhaps getting seventy-five sen's worth for fifty sen means a great deal to people like that."

Kenzō found it hard to believe that such people really existed. Of course they would have been equally incredulous had they seen him frenziedly taking notes in that shriveled handwriting of his. "Why must she go on associating with the likes of them? It's all so pointless."

"It may seem pointless to us, but perhaps it doesn't when you have to live in that sort of world."

Kenzō was reminded of the thirty yen he had recently made on the side. About a month before, a friend who ran a magazine had asked him for a contribution. He had regarded it as a challenge to be asked to write something so unrelated to his work, and with the enthusiasm and sense of freedom of a novice had written a rather long piece. And when the friend had unexpectedly presented him with an honorarium, he had been terribly pleased.

The bleakness of the living room had been bothering him for some time. With the money, then, he had immediately gone to a cabinetmaker in Dangozaka, who specialized in rare woods, to have a frame of rosewood made. Into the frame he put a stone rubbing, one of a collection supposedly dating from the Northern Wei, which a friend had brought back for him from China. He attached this to a slender rod of speckled bamboo by means of a ring and hung it on the wall in the alcove. Perhaps because the round bamboo would not lie flat against the wall, the frame refused to stay still even when there was no breeze.

From Dangozaka he had gone straight to a potter in Yanaka and bought a vase about a foot tall. It was vermilion on the outside, with a large floral design in pale yellow. This also he placed in the alcove, beneath the frame. It was an unhappy combination, for the vase undoubtedly dwarfed and made ridiculous the rather small frame hanging restlessly above. With some hopelessness he had gazed at the newly decorated alcove. But it's better than nothing at all, he told himself—beggars can't be choosers. And with that thought he had managed to console himself.

He had then gone to a draper's in Hongōdōri to buy himself some cloth. "I'll have that one," he said to the sales clerk, pointing at the most conspicuous of the many pieces put before him. It was of a splashed pattern and very shiny, and to his ignorant eyes it seemed the most luxurious. "Isezaki silk," the man called it; Kenzō had never heard of it. "You should have enough, sir," said the man, "for a haori to match the kimono." And with little trouble he talked his gullible customer into buying two rolls of the "Isezaki silk."

During the shopping spree Kenzō had given no thought to others—not even to the baby that was about to be born. Not once did he think of those who were having a harder time than himself. He had forgotten even to regard with distant goodwill the unfortunates of this world.

He thought of his sister now in the light of his own conduct. "I suppose she's admirable in a way," he said to his wife. "She is willing to sacrifice something to meet her so-called obligations. On the other hand, she's a show-off too, don't forget. She'll do anything for the sake of appearances. I wouldn't call that admirable."

"Don't you think she might be motivated by kindness too?"

Yes, Kenzō was forced to admit to himself, his sister was not without kindness. "You know," he said, "she may very well be a less callous person than I am."

87

IT was not long after this that Otsune came calling again. She was as poorly dressed as before, but she must have put on an additional layer of underclothes to ward off the cold, for she looked even fatter this time. The brazier had been lit for the guest, and Kenzō now pushed it toward her. "No, no," she said, "don't worry about me. It's quite warm today." The gentle winter sun filtered through the glass window into the room.

"You're getting rather plump in your old age," he said.

"Yes, I am as healthy as ever, thank goodness."

"You're very fortunate."

"Mind you, I'd like it better if my pocketbook got fatter too."

Kenzō was not so sure that such fatness in old age was indeed a good sign. The more he thought about it, the more unnatural—even uncanny—it began to seem. "Maybe she drinks," he said to himself, in an attempt to ease his mind.

The haori and kimono she had on were very worn. They might have been silk, for occasionally they would glitter half-heartedly in the light, but they had been washed and stretched so often that on the whole they looked like paper. But it was characteristic of the wearer that they should be spotlessly clean.

Kenzō had to admit that this round old lady, so awkward in her stiff clothes, looked as poor as she claimed. "It's rather sad, isn't it," he said, "that we should all be so hard up."

"But if *you* are poor, then who in this world isn't!"

Kenzō had not the energy to try to disillusion her. I suppose she envies me my health too, he thought.

He had not been feeling well for some time. But he refused to go to the doctor or share his worries with any of his friends. His sense of foreboding, having no outlet, would at times turn into outrage: "They did this to me!" Of course, he would not have been able to specify who "they" were, had he been asked.

He looked at Otsune and thought: I am young, I can walk about, so she thinks I am in perfect health; my house has an outside gate, I keep a maid, so I must be rich. He looked past her at the recently acquired picture frame and the vase. He then remembered the shiny Isezaki silk, which would be ready to be worn in a day or two. And he wondered at his own inability to feel any sympathy for the old woman. He tried to tell himself once more that he was perhaps a callous individual, but he was able immediately to add, "And why shouldn't I be?"

Otsune began talking at length about her son-in-law who supported her. What concerned her most—here she was like most people of this world—was what she chose to call the fellow's "ability." By this she meant of course his capacity to earn money. In all these years she had failed to discover any other standard by which to judge a man. "He isn't much, I'm afraid," she said. "If only he would make a little more. . . ."

She didn't call him a laggard, true, but there was malice in the way she told Kenzō how much his efforts brought in every month. If she bought cloth as she judged men, Kenzō thought, she would buy it by the pound, regardless of its quality or design.

After all, no one in Kenzō's profession could afford to admit that money was the measure of a man's worth. With cold indifference he listened to Otsune's complaints.

88

WHEN he thought she had been allowed to talk long enough he got up and went to his study. He picked up his wallet, and finding a five-yen bill in it, took it out. He returned to the living room and put it down in front of Otsune. "Forgive me, but I thought you might want to go back by rickshaw."

"Oh no, you mustn't. I didn't come for anything like that." So saying she picked up the money and pocketed it.

Otsune's previous visit had ended exactly like this—their remarks, even the sum of five yen, were the same.

When she had gone, he said to his wife, "What if I don't have five yen the next time she comes?" Otsune could hardly be expected to know that Kenzō's wallet was not always graced by a five-yen bill. But immediately he began to feel irritated at his own apprehensiveness. "What's the matter with me?" he said. "Why should I feel I ought to have five yen on me every time she shows up? I'm getting as bad as my sister."

His wife went on with her ironing. It's your business, not mine, she was obviously thinking. "If you don't have it, you don't have it," she finally said. "No amount of vanity is going to make five yen suddenly appear, so stop fussing."

"I don't need to be told that I can't give away five yen when I don't have it."

The silence that followed was broken by the sound of the charcoal in the iron being put back into the brazier. Then she said, "How is it that you had five yen in your wallet today anyway?"

Kenzō had paid five yen for the vase that now stood so incongruously in the alcove. The picture frame too had cost five yen. When he was buying it the man had pointed to a beautiful rosewood bookcase and said, "You can have it for a hundred." Enviously eyeing the bookcase Kenzō had handed to the man the precious five yen, now made to seem insignificant by the mention of a hundred yen. He had then spent a little over ten yen on the shiny Isezaki silk. After these purchases, all that had been left of the honorarium was five yen. And now that was gone.

"I was hoping to buy something with it," he said to his wife.

"What sort of thing?"

The truth was, he really hadn't had anything particular in mind. He had simply wanted to go on spending money. "Oh," he said, "this and that, you know."

Having little interest in her husband's acquisitions, past or future, she changed the subject. "That old lady is certainly a lot more in control of herself than your sister, isn't she? Even if she were to bump into Shimada by accident in this house, one could trust her not to make too much of a scene, wouldn't you say?"

"Let's be grateful their visits haven't coincided so far. Those two sitting in the same room—what a thought. One of them at a time is as much as I can bear."

"Do you think they'd start quarreling even now?"

"It's not what they might do to each other that worries me. I'm thinking of my own comfort."

"Neither seems to know that the other comes here, do they?"

"I wonder."

Shimada had never mentioned Otsune, and contrary to Kenzō's expectations, Otsune had never mentioned Shimada either.

"She's on the whole a better person than that man, don't you think?"

"Why?"

"Well, when you give her five yen, she goes home quite happy."

True enough, when compared to Shimada, whose greed, it seemed, knew no bounds, Otsune did seem rather uncomplicated and docile.

89

SOON afterward Shimada appeared. As Kenzō looked at the face with the long upper lip he thought: Even he and Otsune must at one time have been happy together; what pleasurable excitement they must have shared as they watched their savings pile up, paying no heed to others' jokes about their lighting their fingernail clippings and so on; they must have looked forward to a happy future, whatever that might have meant to them; and now, even the money, which would have been the one meaningful souvenir of their happy days together, was gone; what did they think as they remembered the past which had left them with nothing?

Kenzō was about to say something about Otsune; but when he saw Shimada's dull face totally without any sign of longing or remembrance, he lost the urge. It was as though when the money disappeared from his life, all his old animosities and attachments went with it.

Shimada brought out his tobacco pouch and filled his pipe. It needed cleaning, for it made a wet sound as he smoked it. He knocked out the ashes into the palm of his left hand rather than into the brazier. Silently, he proceeded to search for something in his pocket; then he turned to Kenzō and said, "Would you let me have some paper? The pipe needs cleaning."

He rolled the writing paper Kenzō gave him, pushed it into the stem, and twisted it around a couple of times. He was a man who could do such things very deftly. He filled his pipe again and lit it. Puffing away contentedly he spoke at last to Kenzō, who had been watching carefully all the while: "Now that we're near the end of the year, you must be very busy."

"With my kind of work, it doesn't matter what time of the year it is—it's always the same."

"You're luckier than most of us, then." Shimada was about to say something else when the baby started crying in the next room. "That sounds like a baby."

"Yes. It was born quite recently."

"Well, well. Is it a boy or a girl?"

"A girl."

"Is that so. How many do you have now?"

Shimada continued asking questions, not having the faintest idea what his unenthusiastic host was thinking.

Kenzō had read in a European journal only a few days before an article which tried to prove that an increase in the birth rate was always accompanied by a corresponding increase in the death rate. Did it mean, he now wondered idly, that every time a child was born an old man would die? It was a passing fancy, wild and irresponsible; nevertheless he was pleased to pursue it. "In the place of a newborn child, someone has to die." He was like a man having a dream, like a man momentarily caught in a world of fantasy. Had he been more lucid, more intellectually awake, that "someone" would naturally have taken the shape of the child's mother, or perhaps even the father. But in his present mood, he could put only the old man sitting in front of him in the sacrificial role. Considering the meaninglessness of the man's existence, who would indeed be a more appropriate candidate?

"What right has he to be so healthy?" The cruelty of such a thought had ceased to worry Kenzō at this point. "And what did I ever do to deserve my poor health?"

He heard Shimada say, "Onui died, did you know? The funeral was some time ago."

Kenzō had known that Onui would not recover. But the news of her death affected him deeply. "I am very sorry," he said.

Shimada calmly went on smoking. "We all knew she was going to die anyway," he said. So why make a big thing of it, he might have added.

90

OF far greater concern to Shimada than Onui's death was the effect it would have on his livelihood. What Kenzō had long feared now became a reality. "I have a serious problem," Shimada said, "which I must discuss with you, if you don't mind." His face was tense as he stopped and looked at Kenzō.

Kenzō had no need to be told any more. "It's about money again, I suppose," he said.

"Quite right. With Onui dead, Ofuji has no claim on Shibano. He's stopped sending us our monthly allowance, don't you see." His manner, which had suddenly become familiar, was once more respectful as he added, "He used to send us at least the extra pay which came with his war medal. We came to count on it, and to have it suddenly taken away has been an unexpected blow, I'm afraid." He paused, then began again, this time in a more threatening tone, "You are the only one that can help us. You've got to do something, understand?"

"It will do you no good to push me," Kenzō said. "You are nothing to me now."

The sly, probing look Shimada gave him—as though to determine whether or not he could be frightened—made him all the more angry. "All right then," Shimada said, sensing Kenzō's temper and becoming more cautious, "let's talk about long-term arrangements another time. But at least help me out of this present emergency."

Kenzō was not quite sure what Shimada meant by "emergency."

"Everybody needs money at the end of the year," Shimada continued. "That we too should want an extra hundred or two is quite natural, wouldn't you say?"

Kenzō never felt less sympathetic toward the man. "I don't have that kind of money," he said.

"You can't fool me. I know very well you've got money to spare. Look at this house."

"Think what you like. I'm telling you I don't have it because I don't."

"All right, let me ask you this: is it true you get eight hundred yen a month?"

It was incredible. More shocked than angry, Kenzō said, "What I make is my business—it has nothing to do with you."

Kenzō's answer was apparently not quite what Shimada had expected. Not being half so bright as he was impudent, he was now at a loss as to how to handle his opponent. After a brief pause he said, "So you won't help me, no matter how hard up I am?"

"That's right. I won't give you a penny."

Shimada stood up and walked out of the room. As he stepped outside the house and was about to close the front door behind him he turned around and looked up at Kenzō, who stood silently in the hall. "I'll never come to this house again," he said. His eyes shone in the dark. With no sense of uneasiness or fear Kenzō stared back. The disgust and anger he felt afforded him ample protection against the other's hatred.

In her reserved way his wife was watchful and curious. "What happened?"

"I just don't care a damn."

"He asked for money again, did he?"

"I won't give him a penny—ever."

She smiled and gave him a brief sidelong glance. "The old woman plays a much safer game with you, doesn't she? Her demands are modest, so she'll last a lot longer."

"Shimada isn't through with us yet, don't worry," Kenzō said. He imagined his next encounter with him, and felt sick.

91

*A*GAIN he remembered his childhood, for a while forgotten. With the sharp pitiless vision of a man who is suddenly made to see what he had never seen before, he cast his eyes on that point in the distant past when he was sent back to his parents.

To his father he was simply a nuisance. He would look sometimes at the boy as though he could not quite understand how such a mistake had been made. Kenzō was hardly a child to him; rather, he was some animate object that had forced its way into his household. And the love that was in Kenzō's expectant heart was brutally pulled out by the roots and left to wither in the cold. When Kenzō was still with Shimada his father had been so different; he had always smiled at him in Shimada's and Otsune's presence. But now Kenzō was a burden foisted on him; and the smiles were replaced by scowls. The sudden change in his father at first shocked him; then it exasperated him. But he was still too young, too busy growing up, to be disillusioned; his boyish spirit refused to succumb, and he managed to grow to adolescence without knowing true melancholy.

With too many children to take care of already, Kenzō's father was very reluctant to assume any responsibility for him. He had taken the boy back only because he was his son; he would feed him, but he was not going to spend a penny on him if he could help it. After all, he had thought that the boy was off his hands for good.

Besides, Shimada saw to it that Kenzō remained legally his adopted son. From his father's point of view, then, Kenzō was a bad risk, for what was the point of spending money on the lad when Shimada could come and take him away any time he wished? I'll feed him if I must, was his attitude, but let Shimada take care of the rest—it's his business.

Shimada was no less selfish. He was content to stand by and allow the situation to continue as long as it suited him. They won't let him starve, he assured himself; when he's old enough to earn some money, I'll get him back, even if it means going to court.

Kenzō had no home, either in the sea or in the hills. A wandering creature that belonged nowhere, he found his food sometimes in the water and sometimes on land.

To his father and to Shimada both, he was not a person. To the former he was no more than an unwanted piece of furniture; to the latter, he was some kind of investment that might prove profitable at a later date.

Shimada once said when Kenzō was visiting him, "Remember, I may take you back any day now and make you get a job as an office boy or something." Shocked, Kenzō fled. Albeit briefly and vaguely, he understood the meaning of cruelty and was afraid. He was old enough then—exactly how old, he could not now remember—to be ambitious; he wanted to study hard and become important. "I'm damned if I'll be an office boy," he told himself several times. And indeed, he never did become one.

As he remembered those years, he could not help wondering: "How did I ever manage to become what I am now?" He really did wonder; but there was conceit in the question, for it not only suggested a pride in having overcome his environment but assumed also that what he was now was what he had wanted to become.

He noted the contrast between the past and the present. He wondered at how such a past could have developed into such a present. But he failed to note that it was in the present that he suffered.

He had fought with Shimada, he had continued to hate Otsune, he had moved away from his brother and sister and from his father-in-law—all because of what he was now. He had survived to the present, it was true; but in a sense one could pity this man who had in the process of surviving turned himself into what he was.

92

*H*IS wife said to him, "There isn't anybody in this world you approve of, is there? Everybody is a fool as far as you're concerned."

Kenzō was far too insecure to be able to accept such criticism with equanimity. Always touchy and intolerant, he had been made more so by his recent experiences. "So long as a man is what you call 'useful,' you're perfectly happy—isn't that so?"

"What's wrong with that? I should have thought any self-respecting man would want to be useful."

Her father, alas, was an eminently "useful" man. And her younger brother had never wanted to be anything else. A man more unlike them in this respect than Kenzō, then, she could hardly have married.

He was not the slightest help when they moved house. During spring cleaning, he would nonchalantly remove himself from the scene and let the others do all the work. He didn't even know how to tie a rope around a trunk. He knew that others thought him utterly feeble. But the knowledge only made him want to cultivate his weakness, indeed to flaunt it.

Years before, he had tried to persuade his brother-in-law to join him in the provinces, with a view to educating him. The boy at the time seemed to Kenzō unbearably conceited. He walked about his father's house as though he owned it and treated everybody as his equal, if not his inferior. He had a science tutor who came to the house every day. The boy addressed him as he would a fellow pupil, and throughout the entire lesson would stay sprawled in his seat.

"He's got to improve," Kenzō had finally said to his father-in-law. "I'll take him with me, if you like, and see to it that he's properly trained."

His father-in-law received the suggestion in silence and dismissed it in silence. He seemed to find nothing to be apprehensive about in his son's high-handed ways. The boy's mother and Kenzō's wife were equally unconcerned.

Kenzō was later given this explanation by his wife: "They were afraid that you and my brother might have a row, which would then have made things rather uncomfortable between you and them." Kenzō did not doubt her sincerity. But knowing his father-in-law, he suspected that the real reason might have been put thus: "You may think the boy is an idiot, but he is not. He doesn't need any help from you."

Kenzō did not for a moment question the boy's intelligence. If anything, he thought him much too clever. It was really for the sake of his marriage that he had offered to take on the boy. He had hoped that in teaching him he might at the same time make more clear to his wife his own values. This neither she nor her parents ever understood.

Remembering all this, he could not help saying now with undue arrogance, "Being useful isn't everything. What am I to do with a woman who doesn't even know that?"

Deeply hurt, she looked at him rebelliously.

Later, in a more conciliatory mood, she said, "You really shouldn't get so bad-tempered with me. Try being a little more patient, and maybe I'll understand better."

"But whenever I try to explain, you say I'm just playing with words."

"But you do, don't you see? All I ask is that you don't confuse me with all those complicated arguments. Just say things simply, that's all."

"I'm afraid that's impossible—it would be like trying to teach you arithmetic without ever using numbers."

"But when you argue, I can't help thinking that you do so to beat me down, not to explain anything."

"You think that because you aren't very bright."

"Maybe I'm not, but that doesn't mean I should crawl away every time you come out with some ponderous statement that means nothing."

They were back on that old circle of theirs again.

93

*D*ECIDING that there was no point in talking to him any longer, she turned away and looked at the sleeping baby. Then, as though on impulse, she picked it up.

No arguments, no differences of opinion, came between this flabby, octopus-like creature and her; what she held in her arms was no more nor less than an extension of herself. And unable to contain the sudden feeling of warmth that filled her heart, she proceeded to smother the baby with kisses. Kenzō, as he watched, understood clearly the implication of her actions: "This baby belongs to me, even if you don't."

The baby's face was still a blob, and even now its head was covered only by a few patches of sparse fuzz. One had to be very prejudiced to see it as anything but a monster. "What a strange child we've produced," Kenzō said with feeling.

"All babies look like this for a while."

"I can't believe it. There must be some that look a little more human."

"She'll be all right—just wait and see."

She does seem confident, Kenzō thought, a little nonplussed. But then, he reminded himself, this woman had willingly, indeed happily, given up hours of sleep to take care of the baby. And he was forced to imagine how very much greater a mother's love for a child must be than a father's.

Four or five days earlier there had been a fairly strong earth tremor. Kenzō, a born coward, rushed out of the house into the garden. When he went back into the house his wife reproached him bitterly: "There's no end to your self-centeredness. Can't you think of anyone but yourself?" What she found difficult to forgive was that he had not put his children's safety before his own. Kenzō was taken aback; he had never imagined that she would be so angered by what had after all been an impulsive act prompted purely by instinct.

"Do women think of their children even at such a time?" "Of course!" she had answered. And Kenzō had been made to feel very callous indeed.

But now he looked coldly at his wife holding her baby so possessively. "What does such companionship mean?" he said to himself. "Neither understands anything."

He then began thinking of the future of their companionship, and he wanted to tell her: "The baby will grow up before you know it, and will move away from you. You think that so long as you two are together, it doesn't matter what happens between you and me. But you're wrong, you'll see."

He returned to his study and there his thoughts became more academic. "The plantain, once it has borne fruit, begins to wither the following year. So does the bamboo. And what about those beasts that seem to live—and die, for that matter—simply for the sake of their offspring? Except for the fact that their phases are longer, how different are human beings? The mother willingly makes sacrifices to bring a child into the world, and whatever is left of herself she sacrifices so that the child may go on living. If that is her function as ordained by the gods, then it is her right to want her child to belong to her alone. Her possessiveness is not willful, it is simply natural."

He then thought of himself as father; and he saw how different was his role from his wife's. He said to her in his mind, "You find contentment in your children. You have paid dearly for it, and though you may not know it, you'll go on paying for it. Even in your contentment, you're to be pitied."

94

*T*HE end of the year was approaching; and in the cold wind that blew, little snowflakes began to appear. The children were constantly singing "How many more days to New Year?" Their hearts were as eager, as full of hope, as the song.

Kenzō would occasionally hold his pen still and listen to the children singing, and wonder if he too had been like them once.

There was another song they liked to sing—"Oh the miserly rich boss hates New Year's Eve." Kenzō would smile sadly as he heard it, and think that it described his own state no better than the other song, except of course it was perhaps a little more poignant.

New Year or not, he had no choice but to struggle through dozens of students' papers piled up on the desk. As he read each one, he would stop now and then to draw in red ink a line, or a circle, or a triangle against a passage, and at the end he would jot down figures in his small spidery hand and laboriously add them up.

The papers were all written hastily in pencil and in every one Kenzō encountered characters which were almost impossible to decipher in the bad light. Indeed, in the more barbarously written papers, every other character was a mystery. Occasionally he would look up to rest his eyes, and gaze disconsolately at the seemingly undiminished pile.

He put down his pen and sighed in despair. Was this what the English meant by "Penelope's web"?

It was not only his work that never ended. To remind him that there were many other uncompleted things in his life, his wife came in with a visiting card. He looked at it suspiciously: "Who is this, and what does he want?"

"He says he wants to have a word with you about Shimada."

"Tell him I'm not free right now."

His wife went away, and was back immediately. "He wants to know when it will be convenient."

He looked desperately at the pile in front of him. At this rate, he would not be seeing anybody for quite some time.

"Come on," she said, "what do you want me to tell him?"

"All right," he said resignedly, "say I'll see him the day after tomorrow, in the afternoon."

Once interrupted, he could not face the thought of going back to work immediately. Vacantly, he brought out a cigarette and lit it. To his wife who came back into the room he said, "Has he left?"

"Yes." She looked at the grimy papers with the red ink marks, then quickly dismissed them. She could not imagine what a strain it was for Kenzō to read these carefully, any more than he knew what it was like to be kept awake at night by a crying baby. She said as she sat down, "I suppose he's got the usual thing in mind. Won't he ever give up?"

"He's going to squeeze whatever he can out of me before the New Year. What a stupid business it all is."

She was convinced, Kenzō knew, that there was no need to do any more for Shimada. He, on the other hand, was inclined to give the man a little money, if only for old times' sake. But the conversation at this point took a new turn, and Shimada was temporarily forgotten.

"How are your parents?"

"As hard up as ever."

"What about the railroad? Haven't they made him an offer yet?"

"Father seems quite sure they will. But he's hardly in a position to push them."

"Things must be rather difficult for him this time of year."

"Very."

"Pretty desperate, is he?"

"Yes, but what's the use of worrying? It's all fate." Her manner was calm; it was as though she had come to regard everything with resignation.

95

WHEN two days later the man with the unfamiliar name came again, Kenzō was still busily drawing triangles and circles on coarse, cheap paper with a scratchy pen. He went straight to the living room without bothering to wash the red ink stains off his fingers.

Perhaps the man was not exactly of the same type as Shimada's previous emissary, Yoshida, but this was of little significance to Kenzō, who found them equally outlandish.

He had on a striped haori and a stiff sash of the kind favored by shopkeepers. Judging by his manner and his speech, one would not have said that he was a shopkeeper, however; on the other hand, one could not quite take him for a gentleman either. Perhaps he's some kind of commercial agent, Kenzō thought, not knowing exactly what he meant by the term.

Abruptly, without saying a word about himself, the man said, "Do you recognize me?" Kenzō looked at him in surprise. There was nothing distinctive about the man's face; if one had to characterize it in any way, one could only have said that it was the face of a man who had led a very ordinary, tame life. The man smiled smugly, as if he had scored a point. "You don't, do you? No wonder, it's been a long time." He paused, then added, "But I remember you."

"Is that so," Kenzō said curtly, staring at the man.

"You still don't remember me, I suppose? Well, I'll tell you. When Mr. Shimada had the ward office, I was one of the clerks there. You were always up to some mischief or other. Once you took my knife out of the pen box and cut your finger on it. You caused quite a commotion that time, I can tell you. It was me that went and got some water in a basin and bathed your finger." The incident itself Kenzō recalled clearly, but the face had left no trace at all in his memory.

"It was because of our past relationship that I agreed to come here on Mr. Shimada's behalf," the man added. With this brief introduction he proceeded to state the main purpose of his visit—which was, as Kenzō had suspected all along, to get money out of him. "He says he'll never bother you again, so how about it?"

"He promised that the last time he was here."

"Oh. Anyway, why not finish off the whole business nice and clean now, and you'll be spared a lot of trouble later. There'll be no loose ends, so to speak, to bother you the rest of your life."

It's a form of blackmail, Kenzō thought disgustedly. "Loose ends don't bother me," he said. "I'm used to them. Besides, even if I wanted to be spared a lot of trouble later, as you put it, I wouldn't pay money for the privilege. I'd rather put up with a little discomfort than give in to an unjust demand."

The man seemed momentarily at a loss. He rallied soon enough, however. "As you are probably aware, Mr. Shimada still has in his possession that document you sent him when your adoption was formally annulled. Now, wouldn't it be a good idea if you were to get that back in exchange for a sum of money?"

Kenzō could hardly believe his ears. He knew quite well which "document" the man was referring to. When it had been decided that his return to his parents should be entered in the official register, Shimada had insisted on getting a written statement from him. His father, believing that it would be senseless to refuse, had advised him to humor Shimada and send him something in writing, no matter what. Kenzō, not knowing quite what was expected of him, had finally written a very short, harmless note, expressing the hope that they would not henceforth become strangers merely because their relationship had been altered.

With even more contempt than before Kenzō looked at this man who had undertaken to sell such a thing. He said, "That's just a scrap of paper. It's of no use to anybody, him or me. But if he thinks otherwise, he's perfectly free to do anything he likes with it."

96

*T*HE man would not give up. Whenever the conversation reached a dead end, he would stop for a breather, then begin again after what he presumably thought was an appropriate interval. There was no consistency, no predictability, in what he said. It was not as though he would appeal to Kenzō's reason one minute then to his emotions the next; rather, it was simply a matter of his rhetoric being crude and rambling. The end was all that mattered to him; the question of what means he might employ to achieve it concerned him not at all.

Kenzō was at last worn down by his elusive and at the same time obtuse opponent. "You force me to say no when you try to sell me my own peace of mind or that worthless piece of paper. But if you ask me nicely to help an old man in difficulty, and promise that he will never come begging again, I may be willing to dig up some money for him. Only because I once knew him, mind you."

"Yes, yes, that's really what I came here to say. You're absolutely right. So please help him, if you possibly can."

Then why in the world couldn't he have said so in the beginning, Kenzō thought. The man seemed to have a similar thought as he looked at Kenzō. He said, "And how much will you be able to spare?"

Kenzō pondered. He could hardly be expected to know what amount would be appropriate in such a situation. All he was sure of was that he wanted it to be as little as possible. "Let's say about a hundred yen," he said finally.

"A hundred yen? Couldn't you perhaps manage three hundred?"

"I'd give any amount to a deserving cause, which this isn't."

"Yes, yes, I understand—but Mr. Shimada really is hard up."

"So am I, for that matter."

"Is that so," said the man, with a touch of sly disbelief.

"Supposing I told you I wouldn't give you a penny—what could you do about it? If you don't want the hundred yen, say so."

The man stopped haggling. "Well then, I'll go and tell Mr. Shimada what you said. I hope you won't mind if I come here again in due course."

When the man had left Kenzō said to his wife, "I knew it would happen."

"What would?"

"I'm being robbed again. Every time I have a visitor, I lose money. I'm getting fed up."

"The whole thing is idiotic," she said, without much sympathy.

"It can't be helped," he said simply, too tired to explain.

"It's your money—you can do whatever you like with it. Who am I to meddle in your affairs?"

"What money? You know I haven't any!" He flung the words at her, then went into his study. On the desk lay the paper he was reading when the man came. He picked up his pen so that he might continue to deface the already filthy page.

He finished marking the paper. Then it occurred to him that the unpleasant interview with the man might have made him a harsh reader, and so he read it over again, to make sure that he had not been unjust. But even after the second reading he could not be sure that his standards had not changed within the last three hours. Seeking reassurance in the thought that only god could be just, he read through subsequent papers speedily and with forced nonchalance. Even then the pile dwindled remarkably slowly. He seemed to have unfolded and then refolded a countless number of batches, but here he was still, unfolding yet another one. Even patience is beyond us mortals, he thought in despair, and threw down his pen. On the paper he had been reading a spot of red ink, like blood, began to spread. He put on his hat and rushed out of the house into the cold.

97

*H*IS thoughts as he walked the deserted streets were only about himself. A voice somewhere inside him asked, "And what do you suppose you were really meant to do with your life?" He did not want to answer the question, but the voice pursued him and kept on repeating it until he was forced to cry out, "I don't know!" The voice laughed. "I think you know. You know very well where you ought to be going—but you can't get there, can you? You're stuck." "It's not my fault!" He walked on quickly, as though to get away from the voice.

He found himself on a busy street. Like a man waking from a dream, he looked with wonder at the gay, pre-New Year scene. His mood at last changed.

Walking at a more leisurely pace now, he stopped several times to look at the alluringly decorated shops. Even such things as coral or gold-lacquered hair ornaments, normally of not the remotest interest to him, he would gaze at in seeming fascination. "Does everybody buy things at this time of year?" he wondered. He at least did not. And whatever shopping his wife did was not worth talking about. His brother, his sister, his father-in-law— not one of them had a penny to spare; for them all, the New Year was a terrible strain. And of these, his father-in-law was surely in the worst predicament.

Once his wife, when telling him about the difficulties her father was having with creditors, had said, "Apparently they wouldn't have been quite so pressing had he been made a peer." This was after the Cabinet had fallen. Her father's colleagues, feeling guilty about having persuaded him to leave his sinecure post and join the unsuccessful Cabinet, had put him up for the House of Peers. But the Prime Minister, forced to select a limited number from a long list of candidates, had without hesitation struck his name off. His creditors, suddenly turned mean, now began pounding on his door. He vacated his official residence and cut down his domestic staff. Then he gave up his rickshaw. Finally he sold his house. There was nothing more he could do. Day by day, month by month, his situation grew steadily worse.

"He shouldn't have dabbled in the stock market," Kenzō's wife added. "He says that brokers let you make money so long as you're an official. But once you stop being one, they refuse to take care of you, and that's how you start losing money."

"I'm sorry, but what you're saying makes no sense to me at all."

"Maybe not, but it's a fact."

"Don't be a fool. Do you really imagine brokers can make money for you any time they want? I suppose they never lose a penny themselves? Don't you ever think?"

How clearly I remember that conversation, he thought. Then he became aware of his surroundings once more. People walked past him, all of them obviously in a hurry to get somewhere. They looked very purposeful and determined. Some ignored him completely; some threw him a quick glance; and some even looked at him knowingly, as if to say, "You're a fool all right."

He went home and drew some more messy signs in red ink.

98

*T*WO or three days later Shimada's man ap-peared again at Kenzō's doorstep and sent in his card. Kenzō could not very well refuse to see him under the circumstances and once more he found himself sitting face to face with the "commercial agent" in the living room.

The man said smoothly, "I am sorry to bother you at such a busy time as this." But there was nothing in his manner to indicate that he was the least bit sorry. "I talked to Mr. Shimada at length about our conversation. He says he'll accept your offer—he feels he has no choice—but he would like the money before the end of the year."

"But that's impossible," Kenzō said. "The end of the year is only a few days away."

"I know—that's why Mr. Shimada is in a hurry to get hold of some money."

"I would give it to him right away if I had it. But I don't, so that's that."

"I see." There was a brief pause; then the man said, "Couldn't you try? I'm a busy man too, with no time to spare, but here I am, doing whatever I can to help Mr. Shimada."

Kenzō was quite unmoved. What the man did with his time was his own affair. "I'm sorry, but I can't raise the money that quickly."

After another brief pause the man said, "In that case, when may he expect it?"

Kenzō had no idea. "I'll start doing something about it after the New Year."

"But please try to understand the position I'm in. I really can't go back to him at this point with a vague answer like that. Couldn't you possibly set a date?"

"All right then. Let us say by the end of January."

And thus the interview ended, with each man feeling that he had done his best and that he could do no more.

Finding the cold and his fatigue hard to bear that night, Kenzō had his wife make some buckwheat gruel. She sat beside him with the tray resting on her lap and watched him sip the thick, gray liquid. "I've got to find some money again," he said to her. "This time, it's a hundred yen."

"The time to worry is before you make these foolish promises.

Why did you say you would give it to him anyway? You didn't have to, you know."

"No, I didn't have to, but I did."

Kenzō's obstinacy angered her. "There's no point in talking about it, if you're going to be unreasonable."

"Now, that's very interesting. Who would ever have thought that you, of all people, would be defending reason? That's supposed to be my vice, remember. You can be quite a prig, can't you."

"Me a prig? That's very funny. Have you ever listened to yourself talk?"

"Don't you know the difference between being logical and being a prig?"

"All I know is that in you they amount to the same thing."

"Let me tell you something. With me, logic is something that permeates my whole being. It's not merely a matter of words."

"If that were so, your arguments wouldn't seem quite so clever and empty."

"You're wrong. Take the sugary powder that forms on the outside of a dried persimmon, for instance. It comes to the surface from the inside—it's a natural part of the persimmon. Similarly, my arguments stem from convictions deep inside me."

His wife looked at him unconvinced. The analogy, as far as she was concerned, was just another piece of empty oratory. She was not inclined to argue any further. Abstractions not only bored her but demanded more sustained mental effort than she was capable of, and she was impatient to get back to things she could see and touch.

"You're conventional," Kenzō continued, "because it's only what appears on the surface that concerns you. You don't care what's inside a man, so long as he comes to you with easily recognizable labels stuck on him. You look at the labels, you immediately know what you're supposed to think about the man, and you then put him into some ready-made category that's been provided for you. You're just like your father. He's a lawyer by training, and he lives and thinks like one. All he cares about is tangible evidence. Don't let the other fellow get hold of any evidence, is his motto, and you're all right."

"He never said anything of the sort! He isn't at all like that. Neither am I. I am not as superficial as you think. Why must you be so twisted. . . ."

She began to cry quietly. They said no more to each other. The conversation that had begun with Shimada and the hundred yen had somehow got out of control, and ended in this wretched confusion.

99

A few days after that, Kenzō's wife went out of the house for the first time in some weeks. When she returned she came straight into Kenzō's study, still carrying the baby. "I thought I would pay a few year-end calls," she said as she sat down in the warm room. "I hadn't seen anyone for so long." Her cold cheeks were still flushed.

"How were your parents?"

"As usual. They didn't seem particularly worried. I suppose they're past caring now."

Kenzō didn't know what to say. She continued, "They wanted to know whether we would like to buy the rosewood desk, but I said no. There's bad luck associated with it, you know."

The desk, as Kenzō remembered it, was very large, of Chinese make. It was altogether a beautiful piece of furniture. The top was of solid rosewood, with an unusual grain known as "dancing vines." It was easily worth a hundred yen. Her father had accepted it from a bankrupt relative as security for a loan, and now, under similar circumstances, he himself was being forced to part with it.

Kenzō puffed at his cigarette and smiled. "Bad luck aside, where would we find the money to buy something like that?"

"Speaking of money," she said brightly, "why don't you borrow from Hida what you're going to give that man?"

"Hida? Does he have that kind of money?"

"Yes, he does. The company is retiring him at the end of the year, I'm told."

"No wonder—he's long past his prime, you know. But one would have thought that retirement would make him poorer than ever."

"Perhaps it will eventually. But he's rather comfortable right now."

Hida's retirement had apparently been made necessary by the departure from the company of one of the directors, who had been his protector. But his long continuous service entitled him to a sizable gratuity, which would for the time being at least provide him with sufficient funds.

"Anyway, he says he doesn't want to fritter it away if he can help it. Do we know someone reliable that needs money, he wants to know."

"Well, well—so he's become a moneylender at last." Kenzō's sister and Hida had always laughed at Shimada's mercenariness. And now that their own circumstances had changed, how blandly they set about imitating the man! In their unselfconsciousness at least, they were rather like children. "His interest will be high, I bet," he said.

"I know nothing about that. But your sister says that if it's handled properly, they should be able to get an income of thirty to forty yen a month, which would enable them to eke out a living for the rest of their lives."

Kenzō tried to guess the size of the capital from the interest his sister was anticipating. "If they're not careful," he said, "they'll find themselves without a penny. They should stop being so greedy and put the money in a bank. The interest wouldn't be so high, but it would be much safer."

"That's why they want to lend it to someone respectable."

"What respectable man would go to them for a loan? He would be frightened by the mere thought of borrowing money from the likes of them."

"But they couldn't manage, I suppose, if they charged a normal rate of interest."

"Precisely. That's why I wouldn't borrow from them."

"Your brother feels the same way."

Hida had gone to Chōtarō and told him of his plans, and had then asked him to be the first customer.

"What a fool Hida is," Kenzō said. "Just imagine, a moneylender begging someone to borrow from him! No doubt Chōtarō needs money, but he has his standards too."

There was a touch of comedy, Kenzō felt, in the whole unpleasant business. Of course, it was simply another example of Hida's crude self-centeredness, but what made Kenzō uneasy was that his sister should so willingly be party to it. Somehow, the idea of her being related to him by blood began to seem unreal. "You didn't say I might want to borrow from him?" he said.

"Of course not. What kind of a busybody do you think I am?"

100

NO matter what sort of interest Hida charged, Kenzō simply could not see himself borrowing from him. How could he, who had been partially supporting his sister all these months, now go to her husband for a loan? The whole idea was ridiculous. "True," he said to his wife, "the world is full of incongruities, but...." He suddenly wanted to laugh. "You know, the more I think about it the sillier it begins to seem. Ah well, let's not worry about it. He'll be all right, he can get along without my patronage."

"I'm sure," she said. "As a matter of fact, he's already found one customer—some house of assignation or other in the neighborhood."

This is too much, Kenzō thought, and burst out laughing.

She of course felt that her husband could have had a more suitable brother-in-law than a petty moneylender who did business with houses of assignation. But she was not the sort to worry unduly about such things as her husband's good name, and she too began to laugh merrily.

The laughter subsided, and in reaction a mood of depression came over Kenzō. And very soon he was recalling an unpleasant incident in which Hida had figured.

Kenzō had had another brother, between him and Chōtaro in age, who had died of an illness. On several occasions during his illness this brother had shown Kenzō his silver hunting watch and said, "I am going to leave you this." And for almost two months, young Kenzō had greedily dreamed of the day when he would be able to hang his first watch on his sash. How impressed and envious the others would be!

When the brother died, the widow honored the promise and announced to the family at large that the watch would go to Kenzō. Unfortunately, the watch was then lying in a pawnshop and, of course, Kenzō had not the means to redeem it. All he had inherited, therefore, was merely the right to have it if he could.

Some days later the family gathered together again. Without warning Hida brought out the watch and put it down ceremoniously in front of Chōtaro. It was beautifully polished—Kenzō had never seen it so shiny—and tied to it was a new silk cord with a piece of coral at the end. "This is for you," Hida said. "That's right," said Kenzō's sister, "it's for you." "How very thoughtful of you," Chōtarō said. "Thank you very much."

Silently Kenzō watched the three, who seemed hardly aware of his existence, and kept his thoughts to himself. He hated them for the way they had insulted him, and as he watched them gaily chatting away, seemingly unmindful of all the hurt they had caused, he could not help wondering why they had chosen to treat him so cruelly.

And so he had sat through the meeting not saying a word, not asserting his claim to the watch nor demanding an explanation. He had expressed his disgust through silence. And in the end he had found satisfaction in the thought that there was no worse punishment for his brother or his sister than to be despised by someone of their own blood.

"What a long memory you have," his wife said as he finished telling the story. "There's a lot of vindictiveness in you, isn't there? How shocked your brother would be if he knew!" She then looked at Kenzō surreptitiously, as if to measure the effect of her remarks.

Kenzō was unmoved. "Maybe I am vindictive. Maybe I would be more of a man if I could forget. But facts are facts. And even if I could ignore past events, I couldn't very well kill off my feelings, feelings that I had at the time. They will be a part of me always. I could try to get rid of them, but the heavens would never let me."

"All right, all right. All I said was you could borrow money from Hida if you wanted to. If you don't want to, you don't want to, and that's the end of it."

She meant more than she said. She was thinking not only of Hida and the other two as they lived in Kenzō's memory; she was also thinking of herself, and of her parents.

101

*T*HE New Year came. The world had put on a bright new face during the night, but Kenzō looked at it with indifference. "It's all a lot of nonsense," he told himself. "It's a silly little game people play with each other."

What meaning could New Year's Eve or New Year's Day possibly have for him? As far as his own life and immediate surroundings were concerned, this year would be merely a continuation of last year. He wanted to see no one, for even the idea of having to say "Happy New Year" as if he meant it repelled him.

He walked out of the house in his everyday clothes. The New Year smell seemed to linger everywhere. To get away from it, he headed toward the country; at last he was looking at woods and fields made stark by the winter, and thatched roofs and small streams. But he looked with dull, insensitive eyes; even this pretty scene failed to arouse any sensation in him.

It was a gentle sort of day. There was no wind and the fields all round him were covered with a spring-like mist. The sunlight filtered feebly through it and caressed his body. He wandered on, in search of a place where there were no paths, where he would meet no one. After a while he noticed that the ground was wet from the thaw and that his shoes were now heavy with mud. He stood still, gazing vacantly at his surroundings. He then brought out his sketchbook and began to draw. But his drawings were so bad that rather than giving him any peace of mind, they increased his sense of restlessness. He gave up, and proceeded to drag his heavy feet homeward. On the way, as he thought about the money he had promised to give Shimada, the idea came to him that he might try writing something for a commercial magazine.

At last he finished marking the papers. There were still ten days left before the new term began. Resolving to make full use of that time, he picked up his pen once more and started to write.

He was menaced by the awareness that his health was steadily deteriorating. But he paid no heed, and worked furiously. It was as if he wanted to defy his own body, as if he wanted deliberately to abuse it for having failed him so badly. He thirsted for blood, and since others were not available for slaughter, he sucked his own blood and was satisfied.

He finished the task he had set for himself. He dropped his pen, threw himself down on the floor, and then, like an animal, let out a long, deep moan.

He sold his manuscript easily enough. But now that he had the money, how was he going to give it to Shimada? He certainly did not want to hand it over himself. And Shimada, after having sworn he would never come to Kenzō's house again, was not going to relish a direct encounter either. It was necessary, then, to find a go-between.

"I suppose Hida or your brother would be best," his wife said. "They're already involved, after all."

"I'm not very keen to ask either of them, but I suppose you're right. Besides, formally asking an outsider to act as intermediary for something as petty as this would be a little silly."

And so he went to his sister's house in Yotsuya. "A hundred yen!" she exclaimed, opening her eyes wide in her usual theatrical fashion. "But of course someone in your position can't afford to seem too mean. You have a reputation to maintain. Besides, he's rather a dangerous old man, and maybe giving him less wouldn't have been safe." She nodded wisely, pleased with her own perspicacity. "But what a time to ask for money! He's thick-skinned, all right."

Hida, who had so far been lazily reading a newspaper, looked up and said, "Up the waterfall swims the thick-skinned carp."

Neither Kenzō nor his sister knew what he was talking about. But she laughed dutifully, nodding again with a knowing air. She certainly is a lot funnier, Kenzō thought, than Hida's joke.

"But you're a very lucky man," she said to Kenzō. "You seem to be able to get hold of any amount of money any time you want."

Hida was ready with another surprise. "Look at the size of his head! It would put to shame even the great Lord Yoritomo's!"

His facetiousness notwithstanding, he agreed without hesitation to do what Kenzō asked.

102

*I*T was in the middle of the month that Hida and Chōtarō came to Kenzō's house. The pine decorations outside the houses had all been taken off, but their smell seemed still to linger in the streets. The two sat down in the living room and looked around with some uneasiness. It was a room that remained the same no matter what the season of the year.

Hida produced two papers and placed them in front of Kenzō. "The matter is settled at last."

Kenzō picked up one of them and glanced through it. In very old-fashioned language it stated that one hundred yen had been duly received and that the signer would henceforth avoid all contact with Kenzō. Kenzō could not recognize the handwriting, but Shimada's seal was unmistakable.

"In witness whereof we set our seals. . . ." How some people love their whereof's and aforesaid's, Kenzō thought. He said, "I've caused you a lot of bother. Thank you very much."

"It's always wise to have such things in writing. Otherwise, you never know where you are with a man like him. Isn't that right, Chōtarō?"

"Absolutely. Now you can sit back and relax."

Kenzō was unimpressed. He had given Shimada the hundred yen simply out of goodwill. Surely he had never thought of it as the price for being left alone.

Silently he picked up the other paper. It was the one he had written to Shimada at the time of the annulment of his adoption. "In view of the recent formal dissolution of our former relationship, and in view of the payment made to you by my father to cover expenses incurred by you during my stay at your house, I wish now to express my hope that our relationship henceforth will not be marred by inconstancy and unkindness." Kenzō looked at his own words, slightly nonplussed. There's something wrong with the logic here, he thought.

Hida said, "It was his plan all along to make you buy that, obviously."

"That's right," Chōtarō said. "And so you bought it from him for a hundred yen."

Kenzō did not want to talk to them any more.

When the two had gone, his wife picked up the papers and looked at them. "This one is worm-eaten."

"They belong in the wastebasket. Tear them up and throw them away."

"There's no need to do that."

Saying no more, Kenzō stood up and left the room. Later, when they were together again, he asked, "What did you do with the papers?"

"I put them away in my chest of drawers." Her tone was so respectful she might have been talking about some heirloom. Kenzō did not have the heart to scold her, but he was not going to pat her on the head either. "What a relief," she said with feeling. "At least this affair is settled."

"Settled? What do you mean?"

"Well, we have his signed statement now, so there's nothing to worry about anymore. He won't come here again. And even if he does, all you have to do is tell him to go away."

"But that's how it's always been. If I had wanted to, I could have told him to go away a long time ago."

"But we didn't have anything in writing before. We do now, and that makes a big difference."

"So you're relieved, eh?"

"Certainly. It's all settled now."

"But it isn't, you know."

"Why?"

"It just seems so on the surface, that's all. Of course, women like you who take formalities very seriously would think otherwise."

There was anger and skepticism in her eyes. "All right then, what else has to be done before it really is?"

"Hardly anything in this life is settled. Things that happen once will go on happening. But they come back in different guises, and that's what fools us." He spoke bitterly, almost with venom.

His wife gave no answer. She picked up the baby and kissed its red cheeks many times. "Nice baby, nice baby, we don't know what daddy is talking about, do we?"